He was the man in her dreams

The one who had haunted her all these years; the one she put into every book she wrote. Jared was her pirate; fierce, tender, passionate and proud. The shock of recognition made Kate shiver.

"What's wrong?" Jared stirred lazily, turning onto his back. He looked up at her with eyes that gleamed with the banked embers of a fire that had been only temporarily quenched.

"Nothing's wrong. It's just that I've had this odd feeling I know you."

"You do know me. You said I was perfect. Your very words."

She laughed softly. "I'm not sure you can hold me responsible for that remark. I was under the influence of raging hormones at the time."

"If that's the way you're going to be about it, I'll just have to enrage your hormones until you say it again." He shifted, rolling her beneath him. "And again and again..."

"Jayne Ann Krentz entertains to the hilt...."
—Catherine Coulter

JAYNE ANN KRENTZ

THE PIRATE

MIRA

ISBN 1-55166-437-2

THE PIRATE

Copyright © 1990 by Jayne Ann Krentz.

Printed in U.S.A.

For Debbie Macomber,
a generous friend
who doesn't mind sharing a nifty idea

PROLOGUE

"No, absolutely not. You cannot make me get on that plane. I won't go." Katherine Inskip braced herself in her chair and glared at the two women across the small table. Behind her, the glass panes of the airport lounge window vibrated as a jet roared past on the runway, then climbed into cloudy Seattle skies. "There are laws against this sort of thing. This is illegal impressment or something. You can't do it."

"Save the drama for your next book, Kate. You are going to board that plane in fifteen minutes." Margaret Lark, sleek and cool as always, checked the expensive black-and-gold watch on her wrist. Her voice was calm and authoritative. She had spent several years in the corporate world and could still dominate a meeting when the occasion arose. "Sarah and I have discussed the matter thoroughly and we both agree that you need a vacation. Your doctor has told you that you need a vacation. Even your agent said it might not be a bad idea and you know things are bad when your agent thinks you should take a little time off work."

"It's true, Kate. You know it is." Sarah Fleetwood, on the same side of the table and the argument as Margaret, smiled gently, her fey eyes soft with concern. "You're much too tense and nervous lately. You've said yourself that you're not sleeping well. And your appetite is fading. Why, you haven't felt like making pizza or tacos for weeks, and that's not like you. It's the stress. You've got to do something about it."

Kate scowled at her. "So what if I'm a little stressed? I've just come off a ten-day, ten-city book promotion tour. What do you expect? I'm tired, that's all."

"It's more than just jet lag from the tour," Margaret said. "It's been building up for some time. Kate, you've become a workaholic and if you don't take care of yourself, you're going to pay a price."

"What's wrong with being a workaholic? I like my work. In fact, I love it. You know I do. I'm not happy unless I'm writing. I'll go nuts if you take me away from it."

"There's nothing wrong with enjoying your writing," Sarah assured her in soothing tones. "Margaret and I love writing, too. That's not the point."

"Well, what is the point?" Kate demanded, feeling cornered. "I'm happy just the way I am, I tell you. Happy, do you hear me?" She slapped the small table for emphasis. "I've never been so damned happy."

"The point is that you need to start leading a more

balanced life," Margaret announced. "You've been going at a hundred-mile-an-hour pace for far too long. Since your divorce, in fact. You need a break and now that *Buccaneer's Bride* is safely on the stands, you can afford the time to take one. Trust me on this, Kate. When I was working in the business world, I saw plenty of examples of what overwork and stress can do to people. Not a pretty sight." She dug an airline ticket envelope out of her black Italian-leather handbag. "You need to learn how to take time out to relax and enjoy life."

"And Amethyst Island sounds like the perfect place for you to do just that," Sarah announced. Her unsettlingly insightful gaze rested on Kate's set face for a few seconds. Then she reached out and took the ticket envelope from Margaret and pushed it into Kate's fingers. "Margaret and I have looked into this thoroughly. The place has everything: palm trees, warm, tropical seas, a first-class luxury resort, papayas, coconuts..."

"I hate coconuts," Kate pointed out desperately. "You know I do. Remember how I wouldn't eat any of those cookies you made last week because they had those yucky little bits of coconut in them?"

"So you'll eat papaya, instead," Margaret said with a shrug. She glanced at her watch again and stood up, slender and chic in her tailored blazer and fine wool slacks. "Time to head for the departure lounge."

Sarah jumped up beside Margaret, boundless enthusiasm lighting her elfin features. "On your feet, kiddo. You're on your way to paradise and you're going to love it. I just know it."

Kate looked up at her beseechingly and knew she was defeated. It was sometimes possible to argue logically with Margaret, but when Sarah got that expression of intuitive certainty in her deep, knowing hazel eyes, nothing could change her mind. Small, delicate and vibrant, Sarah always made Kate think of a brightly plumed hummingbird. Today, dressed in a lemon-yellow sweater and black-and-white striped jeans, she looked more than ever like some small, exotic bird.

"Sarah, I know you and Margaret mean well, but..."

Sarah took Kate's arm and hauled her to her feet. "Just think of what's waiting for you, friend. You're heading for genuine pirate territory. The real thing. Just like a setting from one of your books. Margaret did the research on this, and she says it's the place for you. You know how accurate Margaret is with her research."

A gnawing sense of fatalism settled over Kate. Sarah was right—Margaret's research was always impeccable. It was one of the things that lent real power to her friend's sophisticated stories of love and intrigue amid the jungles of the modern corporate world.

"And Margaret says Amethyst Island actually has a ruined castle left over from the days when a real live buccaneer lived there," Sarah went on cheerfully.

"A castle?" Kate was intrigued in spite of herself.

Sarah had her halfway down the corridor now, plowing along in Margaret's elegant wake. "This island has a castle on it?"

"That's right. And a history of violence and lust. Just think, Kate, you're going to be able to explore a genuine pirate hideaway. No telling what sorts of bloody deeds were done there in the last century. Think of the atmosphere you'll soak up."

"What is this about lust?" Kate asked.

Sarah waved an airy hand. "Oh, there's some legend about how the pirate king who settled the island went back to England once, kidnapped his bride and took her away to the South Seas. I don't know all the details. I write contemporary romantic suspense, not historical romance, remember?"

"He kidnapped his bride?" Clutching the ticket envelope more tightly, Kate allowed herself to be thrust into the crowd of people milling about at the boarding gate. "What pirate? Which legend? I never heard of any stories about Amethyst Island. In fact, I've never even heard of Amethyst Island."

Margaret smiled and impulsively hugged her friend in farewell. "It's part of a small chain in the South Pacific called the Jewel Islands. You'll have plenty of time to find out all about the place. Have a wonderful time, Kate. When you come back, you'll feel like a new woman."

Alarm flared through Kate as the crowd caught her up and carried her toward the jetway. "Wait. What's this about lots of time? When am I coming back? How long am I to be banished to a tropical island, for heaven's sake?"

"You've got reservations for a month at the only resort on the island," Sarah called out just as Kate got hustled through the doorway.

"A *month*? Good grief, that's forever. I'll be bored to tears. I'll be crawling the walls. I'll be a basket case by the time I get back. And it'll cost a fortune. Neither of you can afford to send me away for a month."

"We put the whole thing on your bank charge card," Margaret assured her.

"Oh, Lord, talk about stress," Kate wailed. "I'll never recover."

Sarah chuckled. "Send us a postcard."

Margaret waved farewell. An instant later, Kate lost sight of both women as she was swept up and carried down the ramp to the open door of the waiting jet.

Back in the departure lounge, Margaret frowned with faint concern. "I hope we did the right thing."

"We did," Sarah said with cheerful certainty as they both turned to walk back through the bustling terminal. "I have a feeling about this Amethyst Island. As soon as you found out about it from the travel agent, I knew it was the right place to send Kate."

"You and your intuition."

"My intuition hasn't been known to fail yet." Sarah halted abruptly in front of a newsstand and grinned at a display of paperbacks.

One book stood out from all the rest on the rack. Its cover, lush and colorful, featured a powerful, good-looking man dressed in a wide-sleeved shirt that was open to the waist to display an impressive chest. A lethal-looking dagger was thrust into his belt. Locked in his fierce, passionate embrace was a fiery-haired woman clad in a diaphanous gown. The backdrop featured a misty view of a tropical island and a ship with billowing sails. The title, picked out in gold, was *Buccaneer's Bride*. Stamped across the top of the book in bold script was the author's name, Katherine Inskip.

"You know what would really make this a perfect vacation for Kate?" Sarah mused.

"Sure. Finding herself a real live pirate and having herself a nice little adventure." Margaret's brows rose and her mouth curved in wry amusement. "But don't hold your breath, Sarah. She's no more likely to encounter the man of her dreams than you or I are. We three may write about romance and adventure for a living, but we live in the real world."

"I know." Sarah shook her head thoughtfully. "But at least you and I still have our eyes out for the right man. Kate has given up looking for him altogether. I wonder if she'd even recognize him if he came along?"

"Probably not. Even if he did happen along, he'd have a heck of a job on his hands just getting her attention. The only men Kate really sees these days are the ones she puts in her books."

"Maybe. But you know something?" Sarah cast one

last glance at the cover of *Buccaneer's Bride*. "I really do have this feeling about sending Kate off to Amethyst Island. Go ahead and laugh if you like, but I think she's in for something more than just a routine South Seas island vacation."

ONE

"What on earth do you mean, hand over my purse, you little worm?" Kate stood in the narrow, cobbled alley and stared in outraged disbelief at the little man wielding the big knife. It was all too much.

She was hot, tired and thoroughly disgusted. Her canvas-and-leather flight bags hung heavily from her shoulders and her camera felt like an albatross around her neck. The purse the little man was demanding so rudely was slung diagonally across her body and bulged with magazines, guide books, cosmetics and a small statue carved out of lava.

The once rakish-looking safari dress was now damp with perspiration and sadly wrinkled from several hours of sitting in a cramped coach-class airline seat. The traveling had become an endless nightmare. Kate was convinced that owing to some oversight on her part during a previous lifetime she was now doomed to travel through this South Seas purgatory forever, never again to know the comforts of civilization.

The little creep standing in front of her waving the knife was definitely the last straw.

"You heard me, lady."

The small, unkempt man reminded Kate of a rat. He darted a nervous glance over her shoulder and then back over his own. Satisfied that the alley was still deserted except for his victim, he motioned with the wicked-looking weapon. "I said give me your purse. Hurry. It ain't like I got all day, y'know."

"You've obviously spent so much time in this heat that you've fried what few brains you've got. Quite understandable. This place is an oven. But pay attention. If I'd wanted to get mugged, I could have stayed home. I have not endured an endless flight, eaten rotten airline food, had my luggage lost and missed my connections just to wind up turning over my purse to the first two-bit thief who comes along."

"Jesus, lady, will you keep your voice down?"

"Why should I keep my voice down?" Kate's voice, already laced with outrage, rose yet another notch in volume. "I have no intention of handing over my purse or anything else to you. Now get out of this alley and leave me alone."

"Now look here, you crazy bitch." The man waved the knife threateningly, but he took a step back when Kate's eyes narrowed. Once more he glanced anxiously over his shoulder. "I ain't got time to be nice about this."

"Neither do I." Kate grabbed her camera and held it up to one eye. She focused on her target and squeezed the shutter-release button. The man's mouth fell open in shock. "A charming pose. You know, if you knew what I've been through today, I'm sure you'd find yourself another poor helpless tourist to rob. I am not in a good mood."

"I don't care what kinda mood you're in."

Kate ignored his interruption. "Furthermore, I am a person who has been under a great deal of stress lately, according to my friends. People who have been under stress are unpredictable and dangerous. You never know what they're going to do." She squeezed off another shot.

"Hey, what are you doin'?" The little man swore and leaped back another step, instinctively raising a hand to shield his face. "Stop takin' pictures of me. What's the matter with you? Just give me the damned purse."

"Very well. Since you insist." Kate let the camera fall to her waist. Grimly, she let the heavy shoulder bags slide to the pavement. She tugged at the leather strap of her purse.

"That's better. Come on, come on."

"This," Kate said through her teeth, "has been the worst trip of my entire life and I've hardly gotten started. I can't wait to get home and tell my friends what they did to me. Here. You want my purse? Help yourself." Kate turned the bulging bag upside down and dumped the contents at her feet.

The would-be thief swore again in a strangled-sounding voice. "You're crazy, lady. You know that? *Crazy.*"

"Stressed, not crazy. There's a difference. If I were crazy, I might actually be enjoying myself."

"What the hell do you think you're doin'?"

"Getting myself robbed." Kate finished emptying the purse. "Come and get it, you little runt."

"Get outa my way." The man edged cautiously forward. "Get back. Go on, get back."

"Is there a good living in this sort of thing?" Kate watched as the man hunkered and worked his way closer to where her wallet lay on the ground.

"Shut up. Just shut up, will you? Don't you ever close that damned mouth of yours?" The little man lunged toward the wallet.

Kate waited until the last second and then kicked out at the hand holding the knife.

"Aargh!"

Caught off balance, the thief dropped the knife and scuttled to one side like a small, startled crab. Kate took a step forward and kicked him again, this time catching the man in a far more vulnerable spot.

"Damn you, you crazy, stupid woman! You're a real nut, you know that?" The man rolled to one side, hugging himself. He lurched to his feet, backing away from her. Then his nervous little eyes flicked to a point behind her. He cursed, turned and fled.

"That's it!" Kate yelled after him, her hands on her hips. "Run like the coward you are. You remind me of my ex-husband, you little twerp."

But the man was long gone. Grumbling, Kate knelt on the cobblestones to retrieve her belongings. It was not a simple task because her fingers were shaking.

"Did you kick your ex-husband around like that?" inquired a deep, amused male voice from behind her.

With a gasp, Kate shot to her feet and spun around. A man lounged in the alley entrance. He was a very large man, a couple of inches over six feet, lean and hard and broad shouldered. Caught in the harsh glare and deep shadows cast by the intense tropical sun, he looked infinitely more dangerous than the man with the knife. The slashing, wicked grin that revealed his teeth did nothing to soften the impression.

But far more unsettling than the dangerous quality was the fact that the big stranger looked eerily familiar. Yet Kate was certain she had never seen him before in her life. She would not be likely to forget those cool silver eyes.

"Who are you? The little twerp's accomplice?" But even as she asked the question she knew this man did not eke out a hand-to-mouth existence taking wallets from innocent tourists. If he chose crime as a career path, he'd go into it in a big way. He'd be a jewel thief or a mob leader. Two hundred years ago, he would have been a pirate.

"The little twerp doesn't have any friends, let alone accomplices."

"You know him?"

"Sharp Arnie and I have encountered each other occasionally over the years. We're not exactly pals."

"Oh." Kate frowned. "Did he run off because he saw you?"

"I believe he ran off because he thought he was going to get stomped into the ground trying to retrieve your wallet."

"I was certainly going to do my best to stomp him. The nerve of some people. Shouldn't we be notifying the authorities or something?"

"Sharp Arnie will be taken care of in due time. Don't worry about him. It's a small island."

"I'll be happy to file a complaint or press charges or whatever one does in this sort of situation."

"Don't bother. We're not real formal around here. Guess I'd better give you a hand picking that junk up or we'll be stuck on Ruby all day."

The man levered himself away from the pink wall and paced toward her. He moved with an easy, coordinated stride that bespoke strength.

He was wearing a pair of faded jeans and an equally faded khaki shirt. The collar of the shirt was open, and Kate realized she was staring at the crisp, dark hair that grew there. She caught herself and came back to her senses instantly as she realized the stranger was reaching for her valuables.

"Hold on just one second before you touch my things. Who are you?"

"Jared Hawthorne. You're Katherine Inskip, right?"

She eyed him warily. He didn't look like a fan who might have recognized her from the photo the publisher put on the inside of her book's back cover. "How do you know my name?"

"I've been looking for you. Billy said you'd gotten

tired of waiting around for your ride to Amethyst Island and had decided to do some sight-seeing."

"Billy being the Billy of Billy's Ruby Island Dive and Tackle Shop? The same Billy who told me that through absolutely no fault of my own I had missed the one flight a day to Amethyst Island? The Billy who was going to arrange for me to spend the night in that fleabag of a hotel on the waterfront until I informed him that if he did not contact the management at the resort on Amethyst Island at once and tell them to send a boat I would be leaving on the next plane for the States?"

Jared Hawthorne winced. "Sounds like the same Billy, all right. He owns that fleabag of a hotel, by the way. But you're in luck. When his message arrived I decided to come over and pick you up."

"I should think so," Kate said. "I'm booked into Crystal Cove Resort for a solid month. The least the resort can do is provide convenient transportation."

"Take it easy. I'm here, aren't I? You've got your transportation. What do you say we get moving? I've got better things to do than hang around here on Ruby."

"So do I. I certainly hope the Crystal Cove Resort offers a few more amenities than Billy's hotel does."

"Crystal Cove offers everything you'll need for a relaxing vacation on a tropical island," Jared said. "Within minutes after your arrival you will discover that time has slowed to an ancient, unhurried crawl and you are in another world."

"You're quoting directly from the brochure, aren't you?"

"Yeah. I wrote it." He leaned down and effortlessly scooped up a compact, hairbrush and several magazines, which he dumped into the empty purse.

"How long have you worked at Crystal Cove?" Kate asked.

"Since it was built. I own the place." He grabbed the strap of one of her flight bags and slung it over his shoulder. "Ready?"

That explained why he didn't have to bother with snatching tourist wallets, Kate decided. He didn't need them. In his line of work people willingly handed over their credit cards. "The resort must have a very small staff if the owner himself has to make the run to Ruby Island to pick up guests."

"Don't worry. There will be plenty of people to wait on you hand and foot at Crystal Cove, madam."

"I don't need a lot of servants, just air-conditioning. It's hot as hell here." Kate picked up one of the magazines and fanned herself with it. "Right now I would trade just about everything I brought with me for five minutes in front of a real air conditioner."

A glint of what might have been amusement lit Jared's silver eyes. "Sorry. Ceiling fans."

Kate blinked. "I beg your pardon?"

"The resort is built to take advantage of the prevailing breezes. All the room have screens and ceiling fans instead of air-conditioning."

"Good grief. You mean I'm going to have to endure this heat for the next month?"

"The afternoon rains cool things off. Nights are balmy. Mornings are pleasantly warm. The heat only gets a little unpleasant during the middle of the day. Smart people stay in the shade or in the water during that time period. They don't run around buying souvenirs." Jared regarded the lava statue with amused disdain.

"I see." Kate snatched the small statue from his hand and dropped it into her purse. "Is it always this hot during the middle of the day?"

"No. Sometimes it's hotter."

"That does it. I'm going to strangle my two best friends the minute I get back to Seattle." Kate hoisted one of the stuffed flight bags and gritted her teeth against the weight.

"Why?" Jared took the bag from her and slung it easily over his own shoulder.

"They're the ones responsible for sending me to this godforsaken place. You know," Kate confided almost wistfully, "I used to have a rather romanticized view of tropical islands. I imagined them as remote, mysterious, exotic locales where anything could still happen."

"What's the matter? Has the image been shattered?"

"You can say that again. I didn't want to take this vacation in the first place, but during the first leg of this trip I tried to be a good sport. After all, my friends meant well. I managed to convince myself I might actually be able to enjoy a few weeks on a tropical island."

"I take it you've changed your mind already?" Jared motioned for her to precede him out of the alley.

"When I discovered in Hawaii that the airline had somehow lost my baggage during a nonstop trip over the Pacific Ocean, I began to change my mind. When I sat in the Honolulu airport for six hours waiting for my bags, I had a few more second thoughts. After I landed here on Ruby Island and discovered I had missed my connection to Amethyst I became seriously concerned. And now, after having nearly been robbed at knife point here in paradise and after discovering that there is no air-conditioning awaiting me at my so-called luxury resort accommodations, for which I am paying a fortune, I realize I am the innocent victim of a malicious joke."

"Don't get paranoid. You're just shaken up from your encounter with Sharp Arnie." A degree of indulgence softened his eyes. "Not surprising, really. That knife of his can be intimidating at first glance. Give yourself a little while to calm down. Just relax."

"Sharp Arnie was merely the last straw. If it wasn't for the fact that I can't bear the thought of getting on one more airplane today, I would turn around and head back for Seattle this minute."

"There isn't another flight out of here until tomorrow."

"And that's another thing I don't like about these remote islands. They're too damned remote."

"Sharp Arnie had a point. Don't you ever close your mouth?"

"Only when I'm working, and I didn't come all this way to work. I'm supposed to be on vacation. Stress, you know."

"Stress makes you mouthy?"

"Among other things." Kate led the way back through quaintly twisted streets to Billy's Ruby Island Dive and Tackle shop where the remainder of her luggage was waiting. She was aware of Jared Hawthorne following behind her like a porter. His dignity did not seem offended, she noticed. He carried the heavy flight bags as if they weighed only a few ounces.

The narrow, sun-drenched streets of the small port village were nearly empty. As Jared had noted, most people were wisely staying indoors to avoid the heat of midday.

Port Ruby was picturesque in its own way, Kate grudgingly decided, but hardly romantic. It was hot, dusty and run-down. An array of ramshackle shops and open-air bars lined the harborfront. Here and there a few dogs of questionable pedigree flopped in the shade of scraggly palms. Everything, including the dogs, looked as though it needed a coat of paint. Kate fervently hoped that Crystal Cove Resort had a bit more to offer in the way of atmosphere.

The door to Billy's shop hung askew on its hinges, the old screen torn and the weathered wood peeling. Kate stepped into the dark interior and breathed a small sigh of relief at the slight reduction in temperature. The now-familiar figure of Billy, who appeared to be somewhere between fifty and seventy and outfitted with skin that resembled tanned leather, stirred from the seat behind the counter. He rose ponderously to his feet, a can of beer in his hand.

"Hey, Hawthorne." Billy's cheerful grin exposed a few missing teeth and some gold ones. "I see you found the little lady."

"Sharp Arnie found her first." Jared dumped the flight bags onto the wooden floor. "He was up to his usual tricks with a knife."

Billy's grin faded. "Sharp Arnie? Is he back on the island?"

"Yeah. Better tell Sam."

Kate glanced at each man in turn. "Everyone seems to be very familiar with Sharp Arnie. If he's such a well-known public menace, why isn't he in jail?"

Billy shrugged. "He winds up in jail from time to time, but mostly he just gets kicked off one island and washes up on another. He makes a sort of circuit around our neck of the Pacific." Billy scowled suddenly as if a thought had just occurred to him. "You all right? He didn't hurt you or nothin', did he?"

"No." Actually, her knees felt quite wobbly, Kate suddenly realized. Delayed shock. Or perhaps it was the heat. Whatever the cause, she wanted very much to sit down. Just wait until she told Sarah and Margaret about this little incident. "Thank you for your concern, Billy."

"Sure, sure. Sharp Arnie usually don't go around stickin' that knife of his into anyone unless he gets real provoked. Don't worry about your wallet. Sam will get it back from him before he kicks the little punk off the island."

"Fortunately, I am still in possession of my wallet. Thank goodness. Imagine trying to notify all those credit card companies from here!"

Billy looked puzzled. "He didn't take your wallet? Hey, that's real lucky, huh? What happened? Hawthorne get there in time to run him off?"

"No," said Kate.

"Hawthorne," Jared said coolly, "got there in time to watch Ms Inskip kick the, uh, stuffing out of Sharp Arnie. The poor bastard was running for cover last I saw him. Ms Inskip was yelling at him and that seemed to be upsetting him."

Billy swung a startled gaze back to Kate and then gave a crack of laughter. "Nice goin', Ms Inskip. Always did admire a woman who could take care of herself. Here, have a cold beer." He fished a can out of a small refrigerator and slapped Kate on the back as he handed it to her.

"Thank you." Kate staggered a bit under the blow but quickly caught her balance. Out of the corner of her eye, she saw Jared watching her as she pulled the tab on the blessedly chilled can. He had that arrogantly amused glint in his silver eyes again, she thought. It annoyed her. *Dammit*, she thought, *why does he look so familiar? I must have seen him somewhere before this. I know this man.*

"Where did you learn to handle folks like Sharp Arnie?" Jared asked very casually as he accepted a can of beer from Billy.

"I took a two-week course in self-defense techniques for women that was offered at my athletic club last year."

"You've had all of two weeks' worth of training, huh? Impressive."

His condescension was annoying. "It was enough, wasn't it?"

"Enough to terrorize Sharp Arnie, I'll give you that."

"A woman on her own has to learn a variety of skills."

"I'll just bet she does."

Kate gulped the beer and sighed. She was not up to sparring with this familiar stranger just now. Her knees felt a little less wobbly, but exhaustion was hitting her like a wave. "When can we get out of here? Right now even a ceiling fan sounds good."

"It does, don't it?" Billy observed, glancing up to where the shop fan hung motionless in the heavy air. "Hopin' to get mine fixed soon. Parts are supposed to be in any day. Ordered 'em six months ago."

"*Six months.*" Kate was horrified. "You've waited six months just to get a broken fan fixed?"

Billy shrugged philosophically. "Island time."

"Speaking of time, we'd better get going. I've got a resort to run, remember?" Jared set aside his unfinished beer and picked up Kate's bags. He glanced casually at Billy. "You want to cut the cards for the fuel?"

"Not on your life, Hawthorne. I ain't takin' a chance on getting stiffed like last time."

Jared shook his head. "I'm disappointed in you, Billy. Where's your sporting spirit? Suit yourself. Put the fuel on the resort's tab."

Billy grinned widely and scratched his stomach. "I'll just do that. Uh, you want me to help you with the rest of Ms Inskip's luggage?"

"Forget it. I can handle these two flight bags."

Billy cleared his throat. "That's not quite all her stuff."

"It certainly isn't," Kate said. "You couldn't possibly expect me to pack everything I'd need for a month in two small flight bags."

"Where's the rest of it?" Jared asked, looking resigned.

"Got it all back here safe and sound," Billy said, heaving two suitcases up from behind the counter. He bent down for a third.

Jared watched the luggage pile up on the counter. "I take it you don't believe in traveling light, Ms Inskip?"

"Blame the two so-called friends who shanghaied me. They did the packing." Kate smiled blandly. "They weren't sure exactly what I'd need, so they packed for all eventualities."

"No wonder the airline lost your luggage," Jared muttered as he picked up one of the suitcases. "The baggage handlers probably got tired of dealing with it and decided to chuck it. Come on, Billy, let's get this stuff on the boat."

"Sure thing, Jared."

"Wait a minute," Kate said. "Shouldn't somebody

be calling this Sam person so he can arrest Sharp Arnie?"

"Plenty of time for that," Billy said, hoisting a suitcase. "Sharp Arnie ain't goin' nowhere."

"What if he leaves the island?" Kate asked worriedly as she followed the two men outside to the dock where a sleek blue-and-white cabin cruiser was tied. The glare off the water hit her full force, and she scrabbled in her bottomless purse for her oversize sunglasses.

"If he's got enough sense to leave the island, good riddance," Billy called over his shoulder. "It'll save Sam some work."

"But if he leaves Ruby he'll only show up on another island. You said yourself he makes a circuit."

Billy chuckled. "If you're frettin' about Sharp Arnie jumping over to Amethyst, don't. Arnie knows better'n to try to work the tourists over there. He tried it once a couple years back and Hawthorne here took him aside and explained he wasn't welcome over there."

"Explained he wasn't welcome?" Kate echoed in disbelief. "I must say the approach to law and order around here is extremely casual."

"Yeah, but it works." Jared tossed her luggage into the back of the boat and bent to untie the lines. "Hop aboard, Ms Inskip. We're ready to leave."

"Not so fast. Just why is Sharp Arnie so willing to spare Amethyst Island?"

It was Billy who answered. "Let's just say Arnie is real respectful toward Jared here. See, Hawthorne owns most of Amethyst. What he says over there goes, don't it, Hawthorne?"

"Most of the time," Jared agreed. "Makes life simple." He leaped lightly on board and reached out to grasp Kate's arm. He hauled her off the dock and into the boat with little ceremony. "Sit down, Ms Inskip." He guided her rather forcefully into a seat and gave her a wicked smile. "Wouldn't want you to fall overboard between here and Amethyst. Something tells me I'd never hear the end of it. So long, Billy. See you later in the week. Thanks for looking after the lady."

Billy grinned. "No problem. Have a nice vacation, Ms Inskip."

Kate opened her mouth to explain once again that so far her vacation was not off to a great start, but she closed it in frustration when Jared Hawthorne rudely gunned the engines.

Abandoning the effort, she sank wearily into a seat and gazed dully out over the water. As she watched, Port Ruby began to shrink in the distance. It occurred to Kate that she could not remember ever having felt so bone weary.

When she got bored with watching Port Ruby, she allowed her gaze to wander back to Jared Hawthorne who was concentrating on guiding the sleek craft through the necklace of small islets that protected Ruby Island from the full force of the sea.

When they got beyond the bits and pieces of land, Kate was suddenly aware of the vast expanse of turquoise sea that lay ahead. She had not spent much time in boats of any size, let alone one as small as the cruiser.

"I assume you're reasonably good at handling a boat?" she called to Jared.

"You'll find out soon enough, won't you?" he retorted cheerfully. Then he seemed to notice the tension in her face. "Hey, take it easy. I make this run three or four times a month. Amethyst is just a short hop."

"I see." The eerie sense of familiarity returned to Kate as she studied Jared's lean profile. Idly she tried to pin down who it was he reminded her of. His hair was dark, nearly black, worn unfashionably long and silvered here and there with hints of gray. He must be nearly forty, she decided. Try as she might, she could not think of anyone she knew who resembled him. Her curiosity overcame her.

"Look," she finally said, pitching her voice above the roar of the engine, "this is going to sound silly, but do I know you from somewhere?"

Jared gave her a curious glance. "No. Definitely not. Believe me, I'd remember if we'd ever met."

"Of course. I told you it was a silly question. It's just that I'm so tired I can't think straight." She ran her fingers through her short hair. The breeze generated by the moving boat was refreshing. "How long until we get to Amethyst?"

"About an hour."

"I think I'll take a nap, if you don't mind."

"Suit yourself."

"Thank you, I usually do," Kate said as she settled back in the shade of the cruiser's canopy.

"What a coincidence," Jared said half under his breath as he watched her eyes close. "So do I, Ms Inskip. And something tells me that could be a problem."

She looked different with her lashes lowered and her mouth closed, he thought, studying her objectively for the first time. More vulnerable, a little softer. Attractive, even.

Damned attractive, if you liked the type.

He decided Kate Inskip was probably only a few years younger than he—thirty-three or maybe even thirty-four. The wide belt of the wilted safari-style dress revealed a slender waist and hinted at full, round hips. The large, button-flap pockets on the front of the dress successfully concealed most of the contours of her breasts, however. That was okay, though, Jared finally decided. A man should have something to look forward to discovering on his own.

A wealth of tawny brown hair styled in a short, sassy fashion made a nice frame for her long-lashed green eyes and tip-tilted nose. It was a strong face, Jared realized, the face of a woman accustomed to making her own decisions and carrying them out, the face of a woman who did not rely on men to smooth her way in the world. But there was an intriguing sensuality about her full mouth, he discovered.

What the hell was he thinking of, Jared wondered in the next instant as he realized with a start where his thoughts were heading. Kate Inskip was definitely not his type. She'd never be his type, not in a million years.

He liked his women soft-voiced, sweet-tempered, gentle and affectionate, preferably with big blue eyes; the old-fashioned type who enjoyed cossetting and cooking for a man; women devoted to hearth and home; women, in short, who reminded him of his lovely Gabriella.

He definitely did not go for the bossy, assertive, independent, prickly little broads who neither needed nor welcomed a man's protection. He was not into modern-day shrews.

Any man who got close to Kate Inskip would have to be prepared for skirmishes and fireworks. She was not a lady who would come tamely to a man's hand. Hell, he'd have to find a way of getting her to stop talking, no mean feat in itself, before he could even kiss her.

Still, that beautiful mouth just might make it worth the effort, he reflected.

The effect of his thoughts on his body made him realize just how long it had been since he'd gotten tangled up with a woman. The fact that he was even taking a second look at this one was proof that it had been much too long. Ms Inskip was right; one of the problems with living this far from civilization was exactly that: it was damned remote and that severely limited the number of his female acquaintances.

Attractive, wealthy, trendy women showed up as guests at the resort from time to time, of course, but Jared had long ago learned that being some rich woman's vacation fling was not his thing. Maybe his reluctance to get temporarily involved with the women who showed up at Crystal Cove stemmed from the fact that he had once been happily married and had learned the comforts of long-term domesticity. No doubt about it, life with Gabriella had spoiled him.

Whatever the reason, he'd never really gotten the hang of casual affairs; never wanted to get the hang of them. He did not like the idea of waking up in the morning with the feeling he'd become one more souvenir.

He studied Kate's gracefully sprawled form more closely. She didn't really look like the type of woman who collected sexual souvenirs, he told himself. Nor did she look like the overindulged, trendy, jet-setter type. She appeared to be exactly what she'd implied she was, a stressed-out businesswoman who badly needed a vacation. The thought was vaguely reassuring.

Then he flashed again on the memory of Sharp Arnie's expression of shock when the little man had finally realized he'd chosen the wrong tourist. Jared grinned. The tale of Ms Inskip's fearless stand in the alley would make a good story, and a good story was always a welcome diversion on Amethyst Island.

When you lived this far from civilization, he reflected, you learned to get a lot of mileage out of old-fashioned forms of amusement.

TWO

Kate awoke in flower-scented darkness.

For a long, confused moment she tried to figure out what was wrong. The bed felt unfamiliar and the soft, balmy air wafting through the room was definitely not coming from her apartment furnace.

In the next moment reality returned, and she rolled over with a heartfelt groan. She was trapped in paradise for four interminable weeks. She wondered if she would survive.

She sat up slowly and cautiously, prepared to sink back into the pillows if the effects of jet lag had not yet fully worn off. But she got to her feet with minimal difficulty and realized she felt infinitely better than she had several hours earlier when she'd collapsed shortly after her arrival on Amethyst.

She had only a bleary memory of what the island and the resort had looked like as she'd trudged up the path from the dock. Glistening white ultramodern buildings elegantly sprawled above a crystal clear cove had been the dominant impression. She'd been blindly following the two bronzed, dark-haired, dark-eyed young men who were carrying her luggage, and as soon as she'd gotten rid of them she'd fallen into bed.

Why wasn't the sun shining, she wondered in growing annoyance as she fumbled her way across the room. Everything felt out of kilter. A glance at the clock showed it was only 10:00 p.m. She had been asleep for several hours but not all night. What she really ought to do was go straight back to bed. Unfortunately she felt wide awake and hungry.

She turned her head and was transfixed by the view of moonlight on water that filled the screened opening on the far side of the room. Fascinated, she crossed the cool bare floors and stood staring out at the silvered sea. Palm fronds rustled softly on the other side of the screen. The fragrance of the night filled her head, and images danced in her brain.

With very little effort she could envision a tall-masted sailing ship in the cove and hear the shouts of its rough crew as it went to work unloading the captured cargo.

She could almost see the figure of the captain. He would be tall and broad shouldered with a lean, strong body and a harshly etched face. High cheekbones, gray eyes and thick, dark hair. Perhaps a bit of silver in the hair for character, Kate decided. Ever since she herself had passed thirty, she'd noticed her heroes had started showing hints of gray in their hair.

A rumble in the region of her stomach reminded her that she hadn't eaten in over twelve hours. Reluctantly Kate turned away from the screened wall and found a light switch.

The room was surprisingly pleasant, she had to admit as she surveyed the spacious suite. The rattan and wicker furniture with its flower-spattered cushions looked comfortable and appropriate in a way it never did when she looked at the stuff in the import shops in Seattle. The dreaded ceiling fan was spinning lazily overhead, coaxing the balmy breezes into the room. There was even a private veranda on the other side of the screen.

It wasn't really so bad.

All in all, Kate decided, she might be able to get through the next four weeks, providing she didn't expire from boredom. Maybe she could entertain herself by working on characters for her next novel. After all, the setting alone should provide inspiration.

Cheered by that thought, she rummaged through her suitcases until she found a jungle print blouse and a pair of khaki slacks. She could only hope that the Crystal Cove restaurant would still be open at this hour. She was starving.

She opened the door of her room and found herself on a narrow, torch-lit path that wound through a garden past other guest-room doors. She followed the gravel walk through lush, heavy-leafed foliage until she came to a small lagoon. Here the path turned and traced the edge of the water until it reached the wide, open-air lobby of the resort.

Lights, laughter, music and a number of hotel

guests dressed in flowered shirts and colorful muu-muus assured Kate she had come to the right place.

She was about to cross the narrow bridge over the lagoon when a small, dark-haired figure dressed in jeans and a T-shirt darted out of a clump of ferns and collided with her.

"Oops, sorry." The boy, who looked to be about nine years old, stepped back instantly and peered up at her. "Didn't mean to run into you like that. I was chasin' my friend, Carl. You okay, ma'am?"

"I'm fine," Kate assured him, aware there was something familiar about the youngster. This time she didn't have to rack her brain for the answer. She smiled. "I'll bet I know who you are."

"Yeah?" The boy looked immediately intrigued. "How much?"

"I beg your pardon?" Kate said in confusion.

"How much do you want to bet?" the boy clarified patiently.

"Good grief, it was just a figure of speech."

"You don't want to bet?" The boy appeared disappointed.

"Well, I suppose I could go as far as a quarter, since I'm so sure I know who you are."

"A quarter? That's nothing."

"Fifty cents?" This was getting ridiculous, Kate decided.

"Okay. You've got a bet." The boy grinned. "Who am I?"

"Are you by any chance related to Jared Hawthorne?"

The slashing grin was a mirror image of Jared's. "He's my dad." There was a wealth of pride in the statement. He immediately dug two quarters out of his rear pocket and handed them to her. "My name is David. How did you guess who I was?"

"It wasn't hard." The combination of dark hair and silver-gray eyes would have been difficult to mistake, Kate thought wryly. She carefully dropped the coins into her shoulder bag. "I'm Kate Inskip."

"Oh, wow." David Hawthorne's eyes lit up with genuine excitement. "You're the lady who kicked the knife out of Sharp Arnie's hand today, aren't you? My dad told me all about it. He said you looked like some kind of lady commando in action. Man, I wish I'd been there to see you do it."

Kate wrinkled her nose. "Lady commando? Your father certainly has a way with words."

"My dad kicked Sharp Arnie off our island a couple of years ago. Ol' Arnie's never come back," David said.

"I'm not surprised. Probably found out he couldn't get a room with air-conditioning."

"Huh?"

"Never mind." Kate smiled again. "Know where I can get a bite to eat?"

"Well, the main restaurant closed fifteen minutes ago, but the bar serves snacks and stuff most of the night. You can get just about anything you want there."

"Thanks, I'll do that. Are you always up and around at this hour of the night?"

"Sure. Except on school nights. But there's no school tomorrow."

"I see."

"Dad says as long as I'm living in a resort, I might as well keep resort hours as much as possible. People stay up late at places like this, you know."

"I see."

David chewed on his lip for a second, looking torn. Then he appeared to come to a decision. "Would you do me a big favor, Ms Inskip? Would you teach me how to do that special kick you used on Sharp Arnie? Dad said you knocked the knife out of Arnie's hand, then stomped him right into the pavement with your high heels."

Kate looked down at the boy. "Is that exactly what your father said? I stomped Sharp Arnie into the pavement?"

"Yeah," David assured her with relish. "Right after you kicked Arnie in the...uh—" He broke off abruptly and coughed. "That is, well, you know. Anyhow, I'd really like to learn how to do that."

The kid was irresistible, Kate decided. Pity the father was such a loudmouth. "All right. One of these days I'll show you how I did it."

David brightened. "That'd be great. Maybe I could show you something in return."

"Like what?"

"How about the reefs? Know how to use a snorkel?"

"I've never tried."

David grinned. "Then we've got a deal. You show

me how to stomp a sucker like Sharp Arnie into the pavement, and I'll show you how to use a mask and snorkel around the reefs."

"Deal."

David nodded, satisfied. He led the way over the small bridge into the wide lobby. "Bar's that way."

"Thanks. Nice meeting you, David."

"See you around real soon." David took off in the direction of the front desk where he greeted one of the clerks and promptly disappeared into a back room. He was obviously very much at home.

An odd way to raise a child, Kate reflected as she made her way through the lobby, but then, she was hardly an expert. She thought wistfully of the plans for children she had once made, plans that had gone up in smoke on the day her husband had filed for divorce. She wouldn't have minded a little boy like David Hawthorne; a child full of life and mischief and the future. But you couldn't have everything, she reminded herself firmly. Fate had dealt her a different hand than the one she had originally intended to play, and she had learned to live with it.

With the ease of long practice, she pushed the emotional images aside.

Her mind instantly zeroed in on another matter entirely. If there was a junior Hawthorne around, there must be a Mrs. Hawthorne. It gave Kate an unexpected jolt to realize Jared might be married. Then she told herself it was hardly an important issue to her.

She glanced at the paneled lobby walls and noticed

that they were covered with several ethereal water-colors. It didn't take a trained eye to tell they were excellent. Which only went to prove that art was where you found it, she thought. She paused to examine two or three of the soft, translucent seascapes and wondered if the artist lived on Amethyst.

After a few moments of scrutiny, Kate made her way into a darkened, thatched-roof bar that hung out over the water's edge. Huge fan-backed wicker chairs clustered around small tables, providing islands of privacy for couples. The tiny candles burning on each table revealed that the lounge was comfortably busy.

Kate quickly located an empty fan chair, sat down and grabbed the small bar menu. A sarong-draped waitress appeared a minute later, smiling in welcome.

"I'd like one of these pineapple-and-rum drinks," Kate said, deciding to be adventurous. "And a bowl of the conch chowder." Was that going to be enough? She was really hungry. "Some of the fried plantains, I think. And how about a salad?"

"Missed dinner?" the waitress asked with a smile as she jotted down the order.

"Afraid so."

"No problem. I'll be right back. Say, are you by any chance the lady Jared picked up this afternoon over on Ruby? The one who knows karate or something?"

"No. You must be thinking of someone else."

"Oh. All right. But I could have sworn... Never mind. Be back in a few minutes."

Kate settled back and automatically tuned in on the

conversations going on around her. It was hard not to listen to others in a restaurant or bar when you were sitting alone. The storyteller in her could never resist listening to someone else's stories.

She did not have to wait long to hear a familiar voice drifting in her direction from the vicinity of the bar. There was no mistaking Jared Hawthorne's deep, dark, amused tones. He was telling a tale and obviously enjoying himself in the process.

"So she turns her damned purse upside down and dumps everything out on the ground. You shoulda seen Arnie's face. But wait, it gets better. She tells Arnie to come and get the wallet, and the stupid little jerk makes a try for it. Then—get this—she kicks the knife out of his hand."

"You're joking." The second male voice had the cultured grace of an English accent. "She kicked him?"

"I swear. Twice. The second time right in the family jewels. Sharp Arnie didn't know what hit him. I wish I'd had a camera. She did, though. She took a couple of pictures of Arnie."

"My word. If that's her idea of a souvenir photograph, she must have a very interesting album at home."

"That thought did cross my mind."

Kate got to her feet as her drink arrived. "Thank you," she said crisply, taking the tall glass out of the waitress's hand. "I'll be right back."

Drink in hand, Kate marched the short distance to where Jared was lounging on a stool. His back was to her as he sat, elbows folded in front of him, one foot casually propped on the brass rail that ran around the bottom of the bar. He was intent on telling his story to the bartender, a square-jawed, balding man who carried himself with a distinctly military bearing. The crisply ironed khaki shirt with its array of epaulets, buttons and pockets added to the overall effect. He was polishing a glass as he enjoyed Jared's tale.

"I'd have given a great deal to have seen the entire affair," the bartender mused, shaking his head in wonder. "What's the lady like? She sounds most remarkable."

"Interesting, but definitely not my type. A real spitfire. Has a tongue that can tear a man to shreds from twenty paces. You should have heard her chewing out Arnie. Took a real strip off him. Even told him he reminded her of her ex-husband, heaven help him."

"Who? Arnie?"

"No, the ex-husband. At any rate, after she'd sent Sharp Arnie running, she started talking about filing a complaint."

"Sam will take care of him."

"That's what I told her. I don't think she was impressed with our brand of local law enforcement, though. She's one prickly little broad, I can tell you that. Not the kind who'd cook your dinner and then fetch your pipe and slippers for you."

"You employ three professional chefs, you don't smoke a pipe and I've never seen you wear a pair of slippers in all the time I've known you. I fail to see the problem."

"Wait until you meet her. You'll see what I mean. A man could get scratched if he wasn't real careful. Ask Sharp Arnie." Jared took a sip from the drink in front of him. "Not bad-looking, though," he added thoughtfully. "I was thinking this afternoon there might be possibilities if you could just figure out a way to get her to close her mouth for thirty seconds or so."

The bartender suddenly sensed Kate's presence. He glanced over Jared's shoulder and his bushy brows climbed. "Short, light brown hair? About five foot five. Nice eyes?"

Jared set down his glass in surprise. "How'd you know?" Realization dawned. "Oh, hell." He groaned and swung slowly around on the stool to face Kate. His smile was deliberately charming. "Good evening, Ms Inskip. Feeling rested?"

"I was feeling much better," Kate murmured, idly stirring her drink with the little parasol that decorated it. "Until I realized I have apparently become a major topic of conversation around here. You folks living on tropical islands must be awfully short of entertainment if you have to resort to gossiping about your paying guests."

In the glow of the candlelight, Jared's starkly carved features looked taut and strained in spite of the smile. Kate was willing to bet he was probably turning a dull red. She wished the lighting was better so she could be certain.

"I was just, uh, telling the colonel here how you

took on Sharp Arnie this afternoon," Jared said carefully.

"I was very impressed, Ms Inskip," the bartender said, sounding genuinely admiring. "Very impressed, indeed."

"In spite of the fact that I'm one prickly little broad?" Kate smiled sweetly and sipped her drink. "In spite of the fact that I can tear a man to shreds with my tongue at twenty paces? In spite of the fact that I can't be relied on to fetch a man his pipe and slippers?"

"Unlike our friend Jared here, I've always admired a female who speaks up for herself," the colonel declared gallantly. "Never did care for lady wimps."

"Then we have something in common. I myself am not fond of wimps, male or female." Kate allowed her glance to flicker assessingly over Jared. "And there is certainly nothing more useless than a man who arrives too late to be of assistance to a lady in distress, is there?"

"Christ," Jared muttered. "You want to dig your claws in a little deeper? Maybe draw some blood this time?"

"Pay no attention to him, Ms Inskip. He's just the boss around here. I hope you will allow the management to buy you another drink. After what you've been through today, you deserve a second." The colonel reached for a glass.

"How kind of you." Kate inclined her head in a gracious gesture. "Have it sent over to the table, please. And do thank the *management* for me, will you? I wouldn't want anyone to think I wasn't properly appreciative."

"I'll pass the word along," the colonel promised on a soft chuckle.

Still smiling, Kate removed the little parasol from her glass and stuck it into Jared's shirt pocket. He didn't move. "Very nice," she said, stepping back to admire the effect. "No home-cooked meal, pipe or slippers, I'm afraid, but don't ever say I lack the feminine touch. Now if you'll excuse me, I'll get back to my dinner." She turned away, pointedly ignoring Jared, who sat grim mouthed on his stool.

"Seems very nice to me, Jared," the colonel remarked loudly enough for Kate to overhear. "But then I've always had a certain appreciation for the feisty type myself. Never boring, you know."

Kate did not hear whatever it was Jared mumbled in response. She was quite satisfied with having made her feelings known. Jared Hawthorne might think twice next time before he entertained others with outrageous stories about innocent tourists.

Kate's full attention was captured by the bowl of steaming conch chowder that awaited her at her table. She resumed her seat, took a last swallow of the pineapple-and-rum concoction in her glass and prepared to dig in. She'd taken no more than two spoonfuls of the chowder when she realized she was no longer alone. It didn't take a great deal of intuition to guess who was impinging on her privacy.

"Here's your free drink," Jared said, looming up out of the shadows to stand beside her table. He put it down in front of her. "I'll have the chowder put on the house tab, too."

Without asking permission, he sprawled gracefully in the other fan chair. Kate noticed he was still wearing the tiny parasol in his shirt pocket. His hooded eyes met hers across the candle flame.

"I suppose you'd like an apology?" Jared said.

He looked right at home framed by the exotic wicker backdrop, Kate observed. The glow of the candle gleamed off his long, dark hair and highlighted his harsh, bold features. The unwavering intensity of his gaze was startling. For a moment she stared at him and saw an island lord who lived just beyond the reach of civilization; a man who could indulge himself by playing by his own rules; a pirate. Frowning, she dismissed the mental image.

"An apology?" Kate considered that. "No, I don't think you have to bother giving me one. Apologies only work when they're genuine, you see. In your case we both know you'd just be offering one out of fear of having insulted a paying guest who might pack up and leave in a huff. You're only thinking of the resort's cash flow. Don't worry, the free drink and chowder will suffice. I'm not going to stage a grand exit just because you think I'm a prickly little broad. I have two brothers and an ex-husband. Believe me, I've been called worse."

"I'm greatly relieved to hear that."

"And don't lose any sleep over that crack about me not being your type, because I assure you the feeling is mutual."

Jared swore softly, his expression one of chagrin. "I'm sorry. I never meant to offend you."

"I know. You were just telling a good story. Don't worry, I understand. Sometimes it's hard to resist the impulse. I should know. I make my living telling stories."

"What kind of stories?"

"I write historical romance."

"Published?"

"Yup."

Jared looked momentarily at a loss. "I don't think I've ever read anything by you," he finally admitted.

Kate smiled brilliantly. "What a pity. One more thing we don't have in common."

"Are you trying to get rid of me?"

"I'm trying to eat my dinner. I happen to be extremely hungry. Stomping knife-wielding assailants into the pavement always has that effect on us lady commandoes."

"Trying to apologize to a prickly little broad has the same effect on me." Jared helped himself to one of Kate's fried plantain slices. "So tell me, Ms Inskip, do all the ladies back in the States take two-week classes in self-defense these days?"

"More and more of us are. How long has it been since you've been back?"

Jared shrugged. "I go once a year to take my son to see his grandparents. That's about it. I'm not too fond of the mainland. I moved out here to Amethyst a long time ago and I've never wanted to leave."

"You like it out here where you get to play king of the island, right?"

Jared smiled slowly, white teeth glinting. "Right."

"What did you do before you built Crystal Cove?"

Jared shrugged. "I was born into the hotel business and I grew up in it. My father was a vice president with one of the big international chains. We lived all over the world. Later I decided to follow in his footsteps. But I soon realized that, although I loved the business, I wasn't cut out to work for a corporation. One day I chucked it all and went out on my own."

He definitely did not look like a corporate animal, Kate thought. "Is your wife equally satisfied with island life?" Kate could have kicked herself for asking, but she suddenly had to know for certain if he was married.

Jared's smile vanished. "My wife died five years ago. And yes, she loved living here. But then she would have been happy anywhere as long as she was with me and David. Gabriella was that kind of woman."

"I see." Kate didn't know what else to say. Jared had obviously been married to a paragon, and now he was alone. "I'm sorry."

"Thanks, but don't worry about it. Five years is a long time. David doesn't remember her and, as for me, I've adjusted."

Kate was very sorry she had given in to her curiosity. She felt as though she had intruded on something very private within this man. Instinctively she backed off, looking for a way out of the overly personal conversation. "I ran into your son a while ago. A nice boy."

Jared's eyes reflected paternal satisfaction. "Yeah, he's a good kid." He paused. "Got any of your own?"

Kate struggled to find another exit. "No. My husband and I talked about it a few times, but he wasn't exactly enthusiastic about the idea. Kept saying we should wait, and then one day he was gone altogether and that sort of changed my plans." She scowled at him. "Are you going to eat all my fried plantains?"

Jared glanced down, apparently surprised to discover the inroads he had made into the stack of chips. "Sorry. Again. I seem to be saying that a lot tonight. Want some more? On the house?"

"No, thanks. I'm finally getting full." At least the overly intimate mood was broken, Kate thought in relief. "Now if you'll excuse me, I'll be on my way." She stood up and reached for her purse.

Jared got slowly to his feet. "Look, if you're rushing off on account of me..."

"I'm not," she said flatly. "I'm rushing off so I can take a walk around the resort gardens. I'm supposed to be doing relaxing things. As I explained to Sharp Arnie, I've been under a lot of stress lately. I'm here to unwind. I assume it's safe to walk around at night?"

"Sure, it's safe." Jared was clearly offended. "You can even go down to the beach. The path is well lit. Just don't try to follow any of the paths that lead into the jungle or up to the castle ruins. They're not lit, and unless you know where you're going you could get lost at night."

Kate's attention was riveted instantly. "There really is a castle here?"

Jared's expression was edged with humor. "Yeah, there's really a castle. But no one is allowed up there except on guided tours. The place is crumbling to pieces and it's extremely dangerous."

"I wouldn't be able to see much at night, anyhow. But I'll certainly want to see it while I'm here."

"We schedule regular tours once a week."

Kate nodded absently, thinking it would probably be far more interesting to explore the place on her own. She had never been enamored of tour groups. "Fine."

"And you'll probably want to see about a costume for the masquerade ball the night after next," Jared added quickly as Kate turned to leave.

She halted and tilted her head inquiringly to one side. "What masquerade ball?"

"In honor of the pirate who discovered this island and built the castle," Jared explained. "The day after tomorrow is supposedly his birthday and the resort makes a big deal of it. We also use his wedding date and the date he arrived on the island and Christmas as excuses to hold the damned ball three more times during the year. The masquerades have become an institution. The guests get a kick out of them. Everyone dresses up in early nineteenth-century costumes."

"I don't have a costume."

"A lot of the regulars bring their own, but for those who don't, the gift shop rents them."

"How nice for the resort's bottom line," Kate observed.

"We try to be a little more subtle than Sharp Arnie, but the goal is similar."

"To part the tourist from his dollar? I understand. I'll check with the gift shop tomorrow. I've never been to a masquerade ball. Wouldn't want to miss anything on my vacation. I have friends at home who will expect a complete report. Good night, Mr. Hawthorne."

"Good night, Ms Inskip." He echoed her mocking formality with a courtly inclination of his head that seemed to suit him.

The Old World grace of the small gesture triggered another fleeting sense of recognition. For an instant longer Kate studied Jared, trying to place him. Then she turned on her heel and left.

Jared stood where he was for a long moment, watching the unconsciously elegant swing of her hips as she walked out of the bar. Then with a small rueful sigh, he headed back to his stool.

"Did you dig yourself back out of that pit you were in the last time I saw you?" the colonel asked as Jared sat down.

"She didn't dump her chowder or the drink over my head, did she? Payoff time, Colonel." Jared held out his hand.

The Colonel sighed and reached into the till for a five-dollar bill, which he reluctantly dropped onto Jared's palm. "I'm not sure you really won that bet fair and square."

"Hey, you can't back out of this, pal. You bet five bucks I'd get the chowder or the drink dumped all over me, and you lost."

"But you did not precisely charm her, did you?"

Jared shrugged. "I wouldn't go that far, but I think I made some progress."

The Colonel poured a glass of whiskey and set it in front of his boss. Then he picked up a cloth and began to polish bar ware with fine precision. "I thought you said she wasn't your type."

"True." Jared took a sip of his whiskey.

"You don't usually get involved with paying guests."

"For a lot of good reasons."

"Granted. So why do I get the feeling you're about to break a few of your own rules?"

"There's something different about this one, Colonel. Something that interests me. I can't quite figure out what it is."

"A man who allows himself to get overly curious about a woman is a man headed for deep water."

"I can swim." Jared raised his glass in an ironic salute. "But as usual, you speak words of great wisdom, my friend."

"And as usual, I'll probably be ignored," the colonel said. "But you might want to watch your step around that lady. You yourself saw what happened to Sharp Arnie."

"Sharp Arnie got what he deserved. But I'll bear your warning in mind."

"Do that."

"Besides, what's the worst that can happen to me?" Jared asked with a nonchalance he didn't really feel. "She's only going to be here for a month."

"What if she doesn't go home when she's supposed to?"

"The tourists always go home, Colonel. You know that. Sooner or later they all get back on a plane and leave."

"What if that turns out to be the worst that can happen?" the Colonel asked quietly.

Jared slanted him a derisive glance. "You worried about me getting my heart broken?"

"Should I?"

"Nope. Like I said, she's definitely not my type. She just happens to interest me, that's all."

"But not seriously."

"Not a chance."

The colonel planted both hands flat on the bar and leaned forward. "Want to bet?"

"You just lost five bucks. Haven't you learned your lesson?"

"Jared, my friend, we both know you've been looking for a wife for the past couple of years. In all this time I haven't seen you get this *interested* in any of the other ladies who've caught your eye. Maybe you shouldn't be so quick to write her off as an unsuitable candidate."

"She said herself we've got nothing in common, and she's right. Take my word for it, Colonel. She'd be all wrong for the job."

"Because she's not like Gabriella?"

"You know, little Ms Spitfire Inskip isn't the only one around here with a big mouth," Jared growled. He was about to change the subject when a movement at the edge of his vision gave him the excuse he needed to end the uncomfortable conversation with his bartender.

He turned his head slightly to watch as a bulky man impeccably dressed in a white straw hat, white slacks, white sandals and a white shirt settled heavily into one of the fan-back chairs. The candlelight glinted on the many rings on the pudgy fingers.

"Butterfield's here," the colonel noted, his aristocratic voice turning cooler than usual.

"I see him." Jared reluctantly pushed himself away from the bar. "Guess I'd better go say hello."

"You want to take him his drink?" The colonel was already pouring out a hefty portion of straight rum.

"Sure. Why not? Save him the trip. You know how Max feels about exercise. Make it a double."

Picking up the rum, Jared left his own whiskey on the bar and made his way through the gloom to the table where the portly man sat. Max Butterfield had removed his hat, displaying a pink scalp surrounded by a fringe of gray.

The overweight man looked up expectantly as Jared joined him. He took the glass of rum and downed a swallow before saying a word. Then he beamed, displaying dimples. "Ah, manna from heaven. Just what I needed, my boy."

"I figured it might be." Jared took the other seat. "Is it still on for tonight?"

"Most definitely, most definitely. I've been count-
ing on this little inspection tour you've arranged."
Max lifted his glass in a toast. "To our successful com-
pletion of this project."

"The sooner it's over, the better, as far as I'm concerned."

"Such impatience, my boy. You must learn to control it. Everything in due course. Matters will be re-
solved soon enough."

"How soon?"

"Oh, I'd say sometime during the next month. The
fish have taken the bait. It's just a matter of time."

Forty-five minutes after she'd left the hotel, Kate
rose from the moonlit rock where she had been sitting
and started slowly back toward the lights of the resort. She thought she would be able to get back to
sleep now, though her body still seemed confused.

It wasn't just her body that was mixed up, she reflected. Her mind was definitely off track, too.

She'd been sitting on the dark beach dwelling on
the subject of Jared Hawthorne, of all things, and for
the life of her, Kate could not figure out quite why. It
was disturbing because the man was clearly not her
type.

She was wise enough to know she did not *have* a
real-life type when it came to men. The man she
longed for existed only in her dreams and between
the covers of her books.

On some intuitive level, Kate had always accepted
that she would never actually meet her fantasy hero.

She frequently joked to Sarah and Margaret that she probably wouldn't like him if she did happen to meet him. He would be too arrogant, too proud and infuriating and much too macho for a twentieth-century woman to tolerate.

When she had eventually decided to fall in love and marry at the age of twenty-nine, Kate had deliberately chosen the sort of man modern women were supposed to covet. Harry had appeared to be a sensitive, supportive, intellectually stimulating male. There had been poetry and candlelight, art films and a shared interest in writing. What more could any woman realistically want, Kate had asked herself.

But things had gone steadily wrong, and after the divorce, Kate had been consumed for a time with a sense of failure and guilt. She knew in her heart she should never have married Harry in the first place. It had been wrong for both of them.

To exorcise the demons, she had turned to the one true love she could always count on—her writing. She knew now that Sarah and Margaret had been right when they said she had allowed her work to consume her these past two and a half years. One needed balance in life if one was to survive and stay sane.

Amazing how clear that was tonight, Kate thought with a smile. Perhaps her friends had been right. A vacation was exactly what she had needed.

Holding her sandals in one hand, she trudged through the sand toward the path that led up from the cove. It was an easy, well-lit walk, and she would have been back in her room within fifteen minutes if she'd stayed on it.

But she didn't stay on it because she came across a fork in the path. One branch was barred with a heavy chain and a sign that warned trespassers not to proceed any farther unless accompanied by an approved guide from the hotel staff.

Kate knew instantly that she had just found the path that led to the mysterious private castle.

There was no way in the world she could resist taking a peek. She was no fool, however. She certainly wouldn't risk her neck exploring the ruins alone at night. But she couldn't see the harm in catching a glimpse of the castle. An old pirate fortress drenched in moonlight was more than any romance writer worth her salt could possibly ignore.

She slipped under the heavy chain that barred the way and managed to get several feet along the steep, dark path before she heard the soft, masculine voices behind her. She froze, recognizing one of the voices instantly.

Discretion, at times, was the better part of valor, Kate decided as she ducked into a clump of thick ferns.

She could not really explain, even to herself, why she decided to hide rather than confront Jared Hawthorne. Kate just knew that in that moment she really did not feel up to defending her reasons for flagrantly violating his edict.

Besides, it would be embarrassing to be chewed out in front of a stranger, and she could hear the second man quite clearly. She was fairly certain that Jared would have no compunction at all about reading her the riot act in front of others for daring to climb the castle path.

The rich, humid jungle scent of the ferns enveloped her as she crouched motionlessly. She smiled as Jared and an overweight man dressed all in white went past within a yard of where she hid. Jared was moving easily, but the portly man was breathing heavily. Kate hugged herself and grinned. She suddenly felt as if she were involved in a small, delightful adventure.

It wasn't until the two men had vanished along the trail and Kate had quickly escaped back toward the resort that she found herself wondering why Jared was breaking his own house rules.

She could think of no reasonable explanation for the owner of the Crystal Cove resort to be escorting anyone up the dark, forbidden castle path at this hour.

THREE

Kate picked up the skirts of her diaphanous, high-waisted gown, adjusted the silver mask that concealed the top portion of her face and crossed the small bridge over the lagoon. She walked into the lantern-lit resort lobby and was instantly transported back to a time and place she had frequently visited in her imagination.

It gave her a disorienting sense of déjà vu. Things looked remarkably familiar, even though she knew she had never walked into such a scene before in her life.

She had stepped into a charming recreation of a Regency-era ballroom. Men dressed in austere black and white circled the room to the strains of a waltz. The ladies in their arms were all wearing low-necked off-the-shoulder gowns that floated around their ankles. Here and there a variety of other costumes added flavor to the colorful mix. Wealthy nineteenth-century planters, pirates, grass-skirted ladies and one or two ship-wrecked sailors bobbed amid the elegant crowd. Everyone wore a mask.

No doubt about it, the costume rental business was a thriving one here on Amethyst Island.

Kate instantly dismissed the exorbitant price she had paid to rent her own lovely yellow gown. It was worth every penny, she decided as she moved into the airy room.

She was asked to dance before she got halfway across the lobby. Smiling, she stepped into the arms of a masked stranger and found herself waltzing for the first time in her life. It was surprisingly easy, she discovered. It was as if she had always known how to waltz.

"This is really something, isn't it? I mean, I came here to go diving, and I end up at a masquerade ball. I almost didn't spring for the costume, but at the last minute I decided to give the thing a whirl." The redheaded stranger grinned beneath his mask as he swung Kate around in a wide circle. "I'm glad I did. Been here on the island long?"

"No." Kate really didn't feel like talking. It broke the spell. She just wanted to drift around the room to the glorious strains of the waltz and pretend she was in another world.

"Diving's terrific around here. You dive?"

"No. I've never had the opportunity. I wouldn't mind learning, though."

"The resort provides instruction, if you're interested. Even if you don't want to go the whole route, you could rent a snorkel and mask. The reefs are unbelievable. It's like being inside a saltwater aquarium filled with the most spectacular fish in the world."

Kate smiled at the man's enthusiasm. "I'll give the snorkeling, at least, a try," she said as they drew to a temporary halt and waited for the music to resume.

"Do that. I'll be glad to show you the ropes. Unless you're, uh, here with someone special?"

"No. There's no one special, but I do have a snorkeling instructor lined up."

"Just my luck. Maybe I could buy you a drink in the bar instead?" the redheaded man persisted.

"Later, perhaps."

"The name's Jeff Taylor."

"Mine is Kate Inskip." She was searching for something else polite to say and wishing the music would start again, when a miniature pirate tugged on her arm. She looked down to see Jared's son, David, in an elaborate costume complete with eye patch and plastic cutlass.

"Hi, David."

"Hi, Ms Inskip. You recognized me, huh? I recognized you right away, too. You look great tonight."

"Thank you. You look pretty sharp yourself."

David glanced at Jeff Taylor and Kate could have sworn she detected a hint of disapproval in the boy's eye. "Seen Dad, Ms Inskip?"

"No, I haven't."

"He's supposed to be around here someplace."

"I'll keep an eye out for him," Kate promised. The more she got to know David, the better she liked him. They had become instant friends. Twice during the past two days he had turned up to chat with her while she sat on the beach in the shade of an umbrella. He'd settled in next to her for some time this afternoon and rattled on about everything from the small island school he attended to his shell collection. He had even taken her beachcombing, and she'd returned to her room with some lovely specimens.

Now David seemed disinclined to leave, though he was supposedly looking for his father. The boy eyed Jeff Taylor again. "So," he said, clearing his throat and trying for a nonchalant pose. "You having a good time, Ms Inskip?"

"I certainly am. Mr. Taylor and I were just talking about the great snorkeling around here."

"Right," David said quickly. "Remember I'm going to teach you how to snorkel."

"I wouldn't mind giving her a few lessons," Jeff volunteered.

"No offense, Mr. Taylor, but you're just a visitor here. I've lived here all my life, and I know the waters around here like the back of my hand."

"I'm sure you do," Jeff Taylor said diplomatically. "But I'd kind of like to show Ms Inskip some of the places I've discovered on my own."

"Perhaps after I've had my lessons from David, I could see some of the reef with you, Jeff," Kate said, making her own attempt at diplomacy.

"My dad could show you the reef," David said quickly. "If you want to snorkel with a grown-up, that is."

So much for diplomacy. "I'm sure he's a very busy man," Kate murmured.

She prayed that much was true. More than once during the past two days she had felt a strange tingling sensation at the back of her neck. When she'd turned around, she'd found Jared Hawthorne watching her with a narrowed, intent gaze. It had happened at poolside and two or three times in the restaurant where Jared apparently ate lunch and dinner with his young son. It had also happened again last night in the lounge. She had gone back to her room, aware of an unsettling sensation of being pursued.

A writer had to work hard to keep her imagination under control, Kate thought.

"I'll bet he could find the time." The boy glanced at Jeff Taylor again and then back at Kate. "Maybe we should go ahead and set a time for the lessons. How about tomorrow morning?"

"Well," Kate began hesitantly. Then she saw the anxious look on David's face. "Tomorrow would be fine."

"Great. It's all settled. Guess I'd better say hello to my friends Travis and Carl. They're here tonight with their parents, along with some other folks I know. They always come to these masquerade parties."

"That's nice. Do you have a lot of friends here on the island?" Kate asked.

"Lots," David assured her brightly. "Dad and I know everyone here on Amethyst."

"I see. I'm sure they're all very nice."

"Yeah, they are. Well. See you later."

Kate nodded. "Goodbye, David."

The boy still looked reluctant to leave her alone with Jeff Taylor, but he finally turned and darted off through the crowd. Jeff chuckled. "I think the kid's got a crush on you."

"Unfortunately, he's a little young for me."

"I, on the other hand, would appear to be just about the right age. Shall we try another waltz?"

For the next hour Kate danced to her heart's content, first with Jeff and then with a very nice middle-aged man who had obviously been wedged into his evening clothes with a shoehorn. After him she found herself in the arms of a nineteenth-century sailor who wore a gold earring in one ear.

Kate lost track after the sailor. The truth was she didn't care who partnered her. She was lost in the fantasy. She floated around the floor in the arms of strangers and imagined herself to be a fine Regency lady who had been kidnapped and carried off to the island kingdom of a wealthy, dangerous pirate, who was secretly the son of an earl.

The man had his reasons for turning pirate, Kate decided, automatically plotting a novel in her head while she danced. Vengeance, perhaps. Whatever the reason, someday he would return to England to claim his title and his estates. But in the meantime he lived a life of violence and elegance here on a tropical island. And he was tired of living it alone. Hence the kidnapping of the lovely lady. How else was such a man to obtain a bride?

At the end of the first hour of steady waltzing, Kate

finally allowed herself to take a short break. Edging through the crowded lobby, she made her way outside into the scented, balmy night.

She just wanted a few minutes alone in the moonlight to catch her breath, she decided, as she moved along the garden path. She was feeling oddly enthralled, almost light-headed. She wanted to savor the fantasy. Tomorrow she would dig out a notepad and jot down all the plot ideas that were occurring to her tonight.

For a moment she thought she was dreaming when she rounded a bend in the garden path and saw the rakish, dark-haired buccaneer waiting for her. He lounged in the shadows of a palm, his wide-sleeved white shirt giving him a ghostlike appearance in the moonlight. He wore a leather belt and gleaming leather boots. The handle of a surprisingly lethal-looking dagger gleamed at his hip. His black half mask shielded the upper portion of his face. The polite inclination of his head was both elegant and arrogant. Kate halted a few feet away.

"I trust you are enjoying yourself, madam?" Jared asked, smiling faintly. He didn't stir from the shadows.

Did he know who she was, Kate wondered. Possibly. She had recognized him instantly, even before she heard his distinctive, rough-textured voice. She realized with a small shock that she would have known him anywhere.

"I am enjoying the evening very much." Kate was

suddenly afraid to move lest she shatter the shimmering magic.

"Did you know the ball is in honor of my birthday?"

Kate regarded him with deep interest. "I was told the ball was in honor of a certain pirate's birthday."

"I never liked the word *pirate* myself. Too difficult to define. One man's pirate is another man's loyal privateer, still another's hard-working sea captain."

"Now I myself have never had any trouble spotting a true pirate the minute I see one," Kate said.

"Have you ever actually seen one?"

She thought of the man who had haunted her dreams most of her adult life, the pirate who existed only in her imagination. "Oh, yes. I've seen one."

"Ah, so you consider yourself an expert on the subject?"

"I like to think so."

"But even experts make mistakes." Jared held out his arm. "Will you walk with me in the gardens, Madam Expert?"

Kate hesitated for an instant, a delicious sensation of adventure making her cautious. The entire evening was beginning to feel like something out of a dream, and though she was in the business of creating dreams she had never before found herself in the middle of one.

But dreams, she was discovering, had a power all their own. On impulse she stepped forward and curled her fingers around Jared's arm.

"Tell me about yourself, my lord pirate," she said

as they began to stroll through the scented tropical greenery.

"What would you like to know?"

"Well, to begin with, why did you come here to Amethyst Island?"

"I think you know the answer to that."

She nodded. "You wanted to carve out your own kingdom."

"There are not many places left in the world where a man can do that. Some men were not born to live in cities or to work for corporations or to answer to others. Some men prefer to live on their own terms and keep civilization at arm's length."

"I can understand that."

"Can you?" Jared sounded intrigued.

"Of course. I write about such men all the time."

"Ah, yes. The heroes of your books. Maybe you do understand. Tell me, Kate, why do you set your stories in the past?"

She smiled. "That's a good question. I'm not certain of the answer, but it's probably because so many modern men seem unsure of themselves, so easily intimidated by strong women." Kate thought briefly of her ex-husband.

"Do you prefer strong men?"

"Most of the women I know prefer strong, centered men. I'm no exception."

"Tell me something, Kate. Do you think you could ever stop doing battle with a strong man long enough to let him make love to you?" Jared asked softly.

"Could you take the risk of letting such a man touch you?"

Kate caught her breath. She looked up at him quickly and was dazzled by the sensual warmth in his gaze. "I'm not sure I should answer that."

Jared gave a muffled exclamation that could have been part laughter and part oath. He drew her closer to his side, so close that Kate's hip brushed his muscular thigh and her bare shoulder grazed his arm. He was a hard, powerful man, and underneath the physical strength was an equally fierce sexuality. She could feel that raw energy radiating from him. It enveloped her, enthralled her, excited her. She sensed the primitive response deep within herself, and the knowledge that she was capable of such a reaction shook her to the core.

"Maybe you're not quite as daring as you think you are," Jared said.

Kate shrugged lightly in the low-necked gown and saw his pirate's gaze drift to the curves of her breasts. She felt suddenly very exposed. The gown was no worse than a swimsuit, she told herself firmly, but that didn't lessen the vulnerable sensation. "Maybe I just haven't had a lot of experience with strong men. There never seem to be very many around."

Jared drew her to a halt in the shadows of a wide-leafed tree that towered over the path. "Women like you are rare, too. Maybe we both have a few things to learn."

She looked up at him and experienced another jolt

of awareness. She was startled to feel herself trembling with anticipation. "Are you going to kiss me?"

"Yes," Jared said slowly, as if he had reached an important decision, "I am. I have to do it. I've been thinking about this for two solid days and it's been driving me crazy."

He bent his head and brought his mouth slowly down on hers. There was no hurry about it. It was as if he was content to take his time and discover all he wished to know about her.

Kate closed her eyes as the compelling fantasy in which she was moving suddenly became as solid as reality. A deep, sensual tug in the pit of her stomach caused her to almost lose her balance. Instinctively she wrapped her fingers around Jared's upper arms, seeking support.

He groaned in response and eased her back against the trunk of the tree. His mouth was warm, strong and searching, and when he moved close, Kate could feel the heat in his body. The fire in him was lighting a blaze within her.

She sensed his hands moving up from her waist, gliding along her rib cage until his thumbs rested just beneath the curves of her breasts. The touch was exquisitely intimate, inviting a response.

Kate parted her lips and surprised herself by nearly panicking for a brief, nerve-shattering moment. The hungry, captivating manner in which Jared took deep possession of her mouth was a revelation to her. She had never had any man's kiss jangle her senses this way. It set off distant alarm bells.

The panic subsided almost at once, to be replaced by a longing unlike anything Kate had ever known. Her arms tightened around Jared's neck, and she whispered his name in a small, choked voice when he freed her lips. She clung to him more tightly and kissed his throat.

"You're full of surprises," he muttered, as if making an important discovery. He nibbled passionately on her earlobe. "A man never knows what he's going to encounter next."

"You're not quite what I expected, either." She pulled slightly away from him, searching his gaze in the darkness.

She could see nothing beyond the glint of moonlight in Jared's eyes. It occurred to her that she was just as well hidden from him. There was something reassuring about the sense of anonymity provided by the masks. It was as if they were both unaccountably free to play this reckless game tonight.

"Well, Madam Expert, what's the verdict? Am I truly a pirate?"

"Yes, my lord, you are. There is no doubt about it."

"Then that makes me an expert," Jared said with a slow smile.

"On what?"

"Ladies like you, of course."

It was Kate's turn to smile. Never had she felt so full of such sweet, seductive, feminine power. It gave her a heady thrill. "Your logic is very profound."

"The way I see it, contrary to your earlier opinion, we do indeed have something in common."

"Do you think so?" she asked with mocking doubt.

"I'm very sure of it."

Without releasing her, Jared swung around so his back was against the tree trunk. He deliberately widened his stance and drew Kate between his legs. The skirts of her yellow gown drifted over his thighs. She put her hands on his waist and felt the hilt of the dagger. She was aware of cold metal under her palm. Definitely not plastic, she thought with a start.

"Is this real?"

"The dagger or me?" He nuzzled her throat.

Kate laughed softly. "Both."

"Yes."

"Where did you get it?" She touched the dagger again as she leaned her head against Jared's shoulder.

"He left it behind when he sailed away from the island for the last time. I found it along with some other stuff in an old chest a few years ago."

"Who left it behind? The pirate who built the castle?"

"Umm-hmm." Jared slid his fingers tantalizingly over her bare arm and dropped a small kiss on her shoulder.

"Is this really his birthday?"

"Yes."

"You said this was your birthday."

"It is."

"You're teasing me. Whose birthday is it really?"

"His. And mine." Jared's tongue touched the pulse of her throat.

"That's too much of a coincidence. What was his name?"

"Whose?"

Kate tugged at the crisp hair that filled the neck opening of his shirt. "The pirate's."

"Ouch. That hurts."

"Tell me his name."

"Such a demanding little creature." Jared lifted his head and looked down at her. Then he caught her face between his strong fingers. "His name was Hawthorne. Roger Hawthorne."

Kate was mesmerized. Her mouth fell open. "Really?"

Jared grinned. "It's the truth."

"You're related to him?"

"The connection is a little distant after all these years, but yes, I'm a descendant. I found out about this island through some old records that had come down through the family. One day about fifteen years ago I chucked everything and came out here to find Amethyst Island."

"That's wonderful," Kate breathed.

"You, my sweet, are obviously a sucker for pirates. But who am I to complain? Come closer and let me show you my dagger." He captured her hand and began to guide it slowly down below his belt.

She pulled her fingers free quickly. "Don't get carried away. I'm not a complete pushover for the species."

"How do you know? You've never met a real one.

The only pirates you know are the ones you invent in your imagination.''

"But I told you I'm an expert." Kate was suddenly tense as the atmosphere became more highly charged. "As much as I may be attracted to pirates, I should warn you that I am not equally attracted to the idea of a vacation fling with one."

The teasing humor went out of him in an instant. "I'm not into flings, either. And as a rule, I don't get involved with paying guests. But I think I'm going to make an exception in your case."

"Is that right?" Kate felt something come alive within her, something that might have been hope.

"Please don't play games with me," Jared said quietly. "We're both old enough and single enough to be able to admit we're attracted to each other. And this..." He stroked her arm in a slow caress and shook his head in silent wonder. "This is something special. I'm old enough to know that, too."

"What happens next?"

"Let's find out." Jared started to kiss her again but halted when a loud, youthful voice called from the garden path.

"Hey, Dad, where are you? Lani says to tell you it's time for the cake. Everyone's waiting."

"Tell her I'll be there in a minute, Dave," Jared called back.

"Okay. Hey, where are you, anyhow? How come you're... Oh. Hi, Ms Inskip."

There was a rustle of leaves and Kate turned in

Jared's arms to see David peering in through the foliage. "Hi, Dave."

"What are you guys doing out here in the bushes?" David asked with the perfect innocence only a nine-year-old can muster.

"I was showing Ms Inskip the Hawthorne dagger," Jared said calmly as he released Kate and stepped out from under the heavy leaves.

"Oh, yeah? It's neat, huh, Ms Inskip? Dad uses it to cut the first piece of cake at these parties."

"That's wonderful," Kate murmured. "It's always nice to see an antique get some use. I was afraid the Hawthorne dagger might be nothing more than a useless museum piece after all these years."

Jared bit back a laugh, his eyes glinting with sensual warning. "I'm a great believer in the old adage, use it or lose it. Come on, you two. Let's go cut my birthday cake." He waited until David had run ahead down the path before pulling Kate briefly close once more. "And as for you, my sweet shrew…"

Kate heard the sexy threat in his voice and shivered with anticipation. "What about me?"

"Just be sure you stick around. When I've finished with tonight's festivities, I intend to show you what happens to smart-mouthed, feisty heroines who can't remember their manners. That crack about the antique Hawthorne dagger is not going to go unpunished."

"You expect me to stick around after a threat like that?"

"How can you resist? You're a feisty heroine, aren't you?"

Ten minutes later, the wicked-looking dagger flashed as Jared took the first slice out of a giant cake. The crowd cheered and champagne flowed. Spelled out in red icing across the top of the cake was the name Hawthorne. Beneath it was a carefully picked-out reproduction of the dagger. Kate stood to one side and sipped from a fluted glass as Jared led a salute to his ancestor.

"The guests love these affairs," drawled a voice behind Kate. "I always said this was a smart bit of theater on Hawthorne's part."

Kate turned to look at the man who had spoken. He was not wearing a mask, but even if he had been, she would have recognized him by his girth and his pristine white attire. This was the man who had accompanied Jared on the midnight walk up the castle path the other night. An uneasy chill chased off some of her pleasure.

"You seem to know a lot about these masquerade balls. Are you a regular guest here at Crystal Cove?" Kate asked. She pushed her silver mask up on top of her head to get a better look at the heavyset man.

"I'm not precisely a guest," he responded judiciously. "More like an old friend of the family. I've been living out here in the islands for longer than I can remember. Even longer than Jared. I'm a writer. Allow me to introduce myself. The name is Butterfield. Max Butterfield."

"Katherine Inskip." Kate racked her brain but

could not think of anything she had ever read by a Max Butterfield. She smiled to herself. Now she knew how other people felt when they were introduced to her and could not claim to have read her books. "I write, too."

"So I hear. Romance novels."

"What about you?"

"I'm working on a novel, but in the meantime I keep body and soul together by doing the odd travel piece here and there. You know how it is."

Yes, she knew. She felt a wave of sympathy for Max Butterfield. She also wondered how long he had been working on his novel. "Have you known Jared a long time?"

"Years." Max took another long drink. "It's a small world out here in the islands."

"You can say that again, Max. Too small at times." The colonel, nattily attired in an early nineteenth-century British officer's dress uniform smiled benignly as he approached. He had an attractive, vivacious woman in her early forties on his arm. She was wearing a gown similar to Kate's in style, but done in mint green. "Ms Inskip, allow me to present my fiancée, Letty Platt. Letty, this is the heroic Katherine Inskip who leveled Sharp Arnie with but a single blow."

"This is getting embarrassing," Kate complained as she shook the other woman's hand. "What did Jared do? Give the story to the local newspaper?"

Letty Platt grinned, her blue eyes sparkling. "Better than that. He just told it to a couple of people, and within an hour it was all over the island. Out here we thrive on interesting tidbits like that."

Kate realized immediately that she was going to like this woman. "I'll keep that in mind. Do you live here on the island, Letty?"

"Oh, my, yes. My husband brought me out here a long time ago when he took a notion to live on a tropical island. He was Jared's mechanic and general handyman for years before he died."

"I see. And you've been living alone out here for some time now?"

"Not for much longer. The colonel and I will be tying the knot soon." Letty beamed up at the colonel, who patted her hand with proud affection.

"Do you work here at the resort, Letty?" Kate asked.

"Officially, I'm the bookkeeper, but in reality I help out where I'm needed. Enough about me, though. I'm delighted to meet you, Kate," Letty confided. "When the colonel told me you were on the island, I was so excited. I've read all your books except for *Buccaneer's Bride*, which I just bought today in the resort gift shop. Can't wait to start it."

"Thank you." Kate felt herself going an awkward shade of pink, as she always did when she met an enthusiastic fan. This was a part of the business she never quite got accustomed to handling. One of the things she liked about writing for a living was that for the most part she could be quite anonymous.

"The colonel says that in addition to stomping Sharp Arnie, you've managed to shake up Jared a bit, and that's great news as far as I'm concerned," Letty confided cheerfully. "It's wonderful to see Jared take an interest in someone like you. He's been very lonely for a long time, though he'd never admit it."

"If you're playing matchmaker, Letty, I think I should warn you you're wasting your time. I got the distinct impression I don't fit Jared's image of the ideal woman," Kate said. Although that certainly hadn't stopped him from making a very heavy pass a few minutes ago, she reflected. Just as knowing what he thought of her had not kept her from responding.

She must have been out of her mind out there in the garden.

"Nonsense. Come with me, my dear." Letty winked at the colonel as she took Kate's arm and led her a short distance away from the two men. She halted and said in a low voice, "I hope you won't take anything Jared Hawthorne says about women too seriously. Like most men, he doesn't really know what he wants."

"I'm not sure we should be discussing this," Kate said uneasily.

"Probably not, but I've already talked to David and I feel obligated to plead his case. He's decided he wants you and his father to get to know each other better, you see. He's quite taken with you. Told me all about how you're going to teach him your special karate trick."

"This is getting more embarrassing by the minute."

"Don't be embarrassed," Letty said. "The colonel is very observant, a real student of human nature, you know, and he says Jared's fascinated by you. The details of that little scene between the two of you in the bar the other night are making the rounds and, frankly, the whole thing sounds delightful. Just like something out of one of your books. I'm sorry I missed it."

"I doubt if Jared found it delightful."

"Nonsense. It's no secret that Jared bases his notions of what he wants in a woman on his memories of his first wife. And it's quite true that Gabriella was an angelic creature. Just ask anyone. But Gabriella died five years ago and Jared is a normal, healthy man in his prime. He needs a woman, and to be quite honest, I don't think he needs another angel."

Kate studied her champagne glass. "Why do you say that?"

Letty smiled knowingly. "It can be hard to live with an angel when a man has as much of the devil in him as Jared has. Enough said, hmm?"

Kate cleared her throat. "Please, Letty, before you get any more ideas, I think I should remind you that I'm only going to be on Amethyst for a month."

"That's precisely why I took the liberty of speaking to you tonight, my dear. There isn't a moment to waste, is there?"

FOUR

"Come on, Dad, you can tell me. I won't tell Travis, or even Carl, honest. You were kissing Ms Inskip under that tree last night, weren't you?"

Jared glanced speculatively at his son, who was sitting at the kitchen table, kicking his sandaled feet and grinning hugely. Behind David the entire wall was open to the morning breezes and a sweeping view of the cove.

"Why do you want to know?" Jared sliced two ripe papayas in half and picked up a lime.

"'Cause. I just want to, that's all."

"Son, you're getting old enough to be told a few of the rules men have to live by when it comes to dealing with women."

"Yeah? What rules?" David was obviously fascinated.

"The first one is that a gentleman never discusses in public what he does with a lady in private."

David's face fell. "That's dumb. Who made that rule?"

"The ladies all got together and made it a long time ago."

"Can they do that?"

"They did it."

Jared squeezed the lime over the papaya and brought the plates to the table, just as he had every morning since Gabriella had been gone. Somehow, without his or David's being aware of it, breakfast had become an important ritual over the years, something they both unquestioningly shared and took for granted.

The other meals were inevitably eaten in the hotel restaurant. Slicing papayas and making toast was about the limit of Jared's capability or interest in the kitchen, though he could make a decent cup of coffee. There was not much point in having three gourmet chefs on the staff if one didn't make practical use of them, he reasoned.

Jared looked at his son's new jeans and realized they were already getting too short. He made a note to buy a new pair soon. Time went by so blindingly fast, even out here in the islands. David was almost ten years old, Jared reflected. There would be more and more of life's hard rules to learn. The trick would be to teach him how to tell the good rules from the bad.

For a moment Jared watched his son stewing silently over the rule regarding women. Then he gave David a wry grin.

"I'll tell you something, kid. If you value your hide, you'll remember this particular rule. Ladies such as

Ms Inskip have a way of getting even with a man who gossips about them."

David giggled. "What would she do to you if you told me about kissing her?"

"I'm afraid to even hazard a guess," Jared said darkly as he sat down and poured himself a cup of coffee. "Probably deck me with one of her karate kicks."

David's humor turned to outright shock. "She couldn't deck you, Dad." He paused, digesting the unthinkable. "Could she?"

A loud, enthusiastic squawk came from the yellow-fronted Amazon parrot sitting on top of its large cage. Jared scowled at the bird. "Keep your opinions to yourself, Jolly." He looked at his son. "Feed your bird. He's turning nasty again."

"Here you go, Jolly." David handed the bird a bite of papaya. Jolly glowered at Jared for a moment and then took David's offering with great dignity. David turned back to pin down his father. "Ms Inskip couldn't really deck you, could she?"

"With any luck I will never have occasion to find out." Jared smeared guava jelly on his toast, wielding the knife with some force.

"Hah. I bet three dollars she couldn't do it," David finally decided. "You're bigger than she is."

"Size is not always a factor, but nevertheless I appreciate your faith in me."

"Are there rules the ladies have to follow?"

"A few. The trouble is, they get to make up a lot of them as they go along." *Such as whether or not they'll*

*still be around when a man comes back to collect what had
been promised with a kiss.*

"That's not fair."

"That's another rule, kid. Sometimes life isn't fair."

"Did the ladies make that one up, too?"

"No. That one got made up without anyone's approval, and we're all stuck with it." Jared bit down hard on the toast.

David kicked his feet while he contemplated that. "I think Ms Inskip plays fair. She's going to show me how to do that special kick today and maybe some other neat self-defense stuff she knows. I'm going to show her how to use snorkeling gear."

"Is that right?" It occurred to Jared that his son was making faster progress than he was. Maybe he should have offered a few free snorkeling lessons. He had certainly gotten nowhere fast last night.

When the cake-cutting ceremonies had finally ended, Jared had looked around and discovered that Kate had disappeared. Like a fool, he had been unable to resist walking through the gardens past her room. Her light had winked out even as he'd stood in the shadows and watched. Jared had spent a restless night, and he was still feeling generally annoyed this morning.

"Yup. We made a deal last night. Some guy she was dancing with offered to show her the reefs, but I reminded her we'd already agreed I'd do it."

Jared looked up. "Who was the guy?"

"A guest. I think his name was Taylor or Tyler or something." David munched papaya, watching Jared out of the corner of his eye. "You know something? I kinda like Ms Inskip, Dad. She looked real pretty last night, didn't she?"

Like a lady out of a dream. "Yeah," Jared said. "She looked pretty last night." And the dream lady had turned into a sensuous creature of heat and shadow when he'd taken her into his arms. But instead of waiting for him after the last dance, she had vanished, the way a dream vanishes in the night. "When are you going to give her the snorkeling lesson?"

"This morning. Right after she shows me some of her self-defense tricks." David finished his papaya and jumped to his feet. He rubbed Jolly's head as he headed toward the veranda. The bird endured the caress with regal condescension. "Gotta go. I'm supposed to meet Ms Inskip in a few minutes."

"Wait a second. You didn't finish your toast."

"I'll take it with me." David snatched up the slice of toast and loped out of the kitchen, out across the veranda and down onto the path that led to the cove.

Jared was left alone with Jolly. The bird eyed him assessingly for a moment and then climbed slowly down from the cage, jumped to the back of David's chair and hopped onto the table to investigate the remains of the papaya.

"What the hell do you think you're doing, you old pirate? You know you're not supposed to be on the table. Get away from that plate or I'll sell a few of your tail feathers as souvenirs to the tourists."

"Wanna bet?" Jolly picked up the papaya in one claw and began to nibble delicately.

"It's always nice to know who's the boss around here." Jared got to his feet and started clearing the table. "Why do you think she ducked out after the masquerade ended last night? I was sure she'd be waiting for me. After the way she responded under that tree, what the hell else was I supposed to think? She wanted me every bit as much as I wanted her, and I know it. I think. Who can figure women? Especially a lady commando with two whole weeks of self-defense training under her belt. Maybe she just got off on proving she could turn me on. I'll tell you one thing, pal. If that's the case, I'm going to put a stop to her game real quick."

"Wanna bet?"

Half an hour later, Jared stood in the open expanse that was one wall of his office and gazed down at the glistening white sands of the cove. From here he could see a smattering of early risers, some with scuba and snorkel gear and some dressed for strolling. At the far end of the beach he saw the two people he was looking for. David was standing on one foot, lashing out toward an invisible target with the other. Kate, dressed in a green maillot, was standing nearby, coaching the boy.

Jared didn't bother to take his gaze off the pair when someone knocked on the office door. "Come in."

The door swung open. "Morning, Jared," the colonel said as he walked into the room. "A fine day, isn't it?"

"Yeah." Jared frowned as he watched Kate demonstrate another quick, striking kick. "But then it always is, isn't it? Come here and watch this, Colonel."

The colonel walked over to stand beside Jared. He peered down into the cove. "Ah. The redoubtable Ms Inskip, I presume?"

"Who else? She's teaching Dave some mishmash of judo and karate."

"The sort of thing she used on Sharp Arnie?"

"Right."

"Nice technique," the colonel observed.

"Too stiff. She needs to loosen up, be more flexible."

"Are we talking about her self-defense skills or something else?"

"Forget it." Jared watched in silence for a few more seconds. "I wonder how she is at baking cookies? Five will get you ten she can't even boil water."

"David doesn't seem concerned with Ms Inskip's possible lack of culinary talents. He appears to be enjoying himself immensely."

Jared narrowed his eyes. "He couldn't wait to get out there on the beach this morning to take the lesson."

"He's becoming quite fond of Ms Inskip."

"I know."

"You don't sound pleased by the prospect," the colonel said.

"She'll be gone in a month."

"That would depend, I suppose, on whether or not she had a reason to stay." The colonel moved over to the desk. "I brought last night's receipts and a couple of bar and restaurant requisitions that need your signature."

Jared didn't turn away from the scene in the cove. "Leave them on the desk. I'll take care of them later."

"Have plans for the morning, do you?" the colonel inquired with a polite tilt of his bushy brows.

"My son is going to give Ms Inskip a snorkeling lesson. Thought maybe I'd supervise."

"Excellent idea." The colonel beamed.

Kate stood, feet planted wide apart in the sand, hands on her hips, and studied David's form with pursed lips. The boy made two more kicks before she nodded in satisfaction.

"Good. You've got the hang of it now. Watch your balance. Balance is everything. It's what gives you the advantage. My instructor said almost everyone is off balance most of the time. The trick is to make use of that fact."

David grinned and kicked out one more time. He accompanied the kick with a loud shout. Then he looked up at Kate. "Think I could take Sharp Arnie now?"

"People like Sharp Arnie are best avoided rather than confronted," Kate said. She ruffled his hair affectionately.

"You didn't avoid him. You clobbered him."

"I was under a certain amount of stress at the time. The smart thing to do would have been to hand over my wallet and run."

"You wouldn't run from anything, I bet. You're

like my dad. I asked him this morning if you could take him in a fight."

Kate blinked. "What did he say?"

"He said he didn't want to ever find out."

"How very wise of him."

"Huh?"

"Never mind. Ready to give me my snorkeling lesson?"

"Sure. I've got all the equipment. You can leave your towel and stuff here on the sand." David bent over to scoop up two masks. Then he glanced down the beach. He straightened almost immediately and waved. "Hey, look, there's Dad. Hi, Dad."

Kate deliberately quashed the little shiver of awareness that went through her as she turned her head to watch Jared stride toward them over the sand. He was barefoot, wearing a pair of faded, low-slung denims and a white cotton shirt. His hair was brushed straight back from his forehead and gleamed in the morning light.

He might be wearing jeans this morning, but he looked as much like a buccaneer as he had last night in full costume, Kate realized. She wondered what would have happened if she'd found the reckless courage to wait for him after the ball. But at the last moment she had known she was not ready for that kind of risk. Facing the Sharp Arnies of this world was one thing; getting involved with a man like Jared Hawthorne was a whole different kettle of fish.

"Good morning, Kate." Jared's slashing grin was a cool challenge. "How did the self-defense lesson go?"

"It went great," David said before Kate could respond. "I can deck Sharp Arnie now, just like Ms Inskip did."

"A chilling thought," Jared murmured, his silver eyes meeting Kate's over the top of his son's head. "Enjoy yourself last night, Kate?"

"Very much." Aware of Jared's intent gaze, she picked up the towel and draped it over her shoulders; the ends covered her breasts.

"I was just curious. You disappeared so quickly someone might have gotten the impression you had gotten bored."

"Not at all."

"No? Then perhaps you just lost your nerve?" Jared smiled thinly.

"It was after midnight and I was tired. Just call me Cinderella." Kate felt something within her rise to his blatant challenge.

"I can think of better names."

"You're right. Calling me Cinderella might imply you're Prince Charming, and we wouldn't want a case of mistaken identity here, would we?"

"Prickly." Jared shook his head ruefully. "Even at this hour of the morning."

"Say, Dad, you want Ms Inskip to show you some of her self-defense tricks?" David asked, impatient with the conversation going on over his head. "She knows all kinds of stuff."

"Are you kidding? You think I want to end up like Sharp Arnie?" Jared demanded.

"Ah, come on, Dad, let her show you. You won't hurt him, will you, Ms Inskip?"

"Oh, I'd be very gentle," Kate promised, her sense of humor getting the better of her. "But I'm sure your father has more interesting things to do this morning than take a self-defense lesson from me, Dave."

Jared's eyes glinted in the sunlight. "Well, I guess I can spare the time to take one short lesson. I have a feeling you know all sorts of tricks, don't you, Kate?"

"Lots and lots," she assured him blithely.

Jared nodded. "I thought so. Including a very good vanishing act. All right, show me something really clever."

Kate saw the taunting laughter in him and was suddenly determined to replace the masculine amusement with respect. She stood facing him, her arms relaxed at her sides. "We'll keep this nice and simple. With all this soft sand, nobody will get hurt. Go ahead, Jared, pretend you're, uh, assaulting me."

"Whatever it takes." Jared didn't hesitate. He walked straight toward her, his hand outstretched to grab her wrist, his silvery eyes alight with mischief.

At the last second Kate wondered if she was being set up, but it was too late to retreat. She glided forward, reached for his arm, pivoted smoothly around and tugged hard just as she had been taught.

It was a textbook throw; much too easy, in fact. Jared came off his feet with no resistance at all and wound up flat on his back in the sand. He groaned once, closed his eyes and did not move.

"*Dad.*" David rushed forward and fell to his knees

beside his father. "Dad, are you okay? Ms Inskip, is he all right? What's wrong with him?"

Kate's satisfaction transformed into instant concern. She hurried forward and knelt down beside Jared. "I don't know. I didn't hurt him. He just took a light fall. I wonder if he hit his head on a rock or something under the sand."

She reached over to check the back of Jared's head and knew she had made a bad mistake when she felt iron fingers circle her wrist. Too late she realized she'd been had. Jared's dark lashes lifted lazily to reveal his wicked anticipation.

"Gotcha."

"You rat." She sighed, fully aware that Jared was going to enjoy whatever happened next.

"Hey, Dad, you were just joking, right?" David's expression skipped from worried to delighted in the blink of an eye. He stood up. "Are you going to show Ms Inskip some of your self-defense stuff now?" He turned to Kate and said proudly, "Dad knows some tricks, too."

"No kidding?" Kate twisted her hand in Jared's grasp and discovered there was no way on earth she was going to pull free.

"I'll be delighted to show you a trick or two, Ms Inskip." Jared rolled over and surged to his feet, dragging Kate up beside him.

"Now, wait just a minute," Kate gasped, aware that pleading was useless but desperate enough to try it, anyway. She was curiously torn between laughter and outrage, and for some odd reason the laughter was winning.

"Hey, Dad, what are you going to do with Ms Inskip?"

"She wanted a lesson, right?" Jared caught Kate around the waist and tossed her lightly over his shoulder. He started toward the water.

"Right," David agreed, trotting along beside his father.

"Put me down this instant," Kate ordered, very much afraid she was wasting her breath.

"So what do you say we give her the lesson she's been asking for since last night?" Jared concluded, ignoring Kate's struggles.

"Don't you dare," Kate yelped as she saw water foaming around Jared's feet.

Jared waded out until he was knee-deep. He didn't seem to care that his jeans were getting soaked. "The first thing you do when you go snorkeling," he said in an instructional tone as he slid Kate down off his shoulder and into his arms, "is get wet."

"You're doing this because of last night, aren't you? This is very petty behavior, Jared."

"I just like to keep the scales balanced. Any man who lets you get the upper hand too often is asking for trouble." He waited three more seconds until the next wave peaked and then he opened his arms and let Kate fall.

The pirate's grin on Jared's face was the last thing Kate saw before the roiling water closed over her head. It was also the first thing she saw when she surfaced again a few seconds later. She managed to get to her feet only to be sent spinning by a wave she hadn't seen approaching behind her. She gasped, kicked forward into shallower water and stood up again.

"Dad, wait, she didn't get a chance to put on her mask," David said, splashing toward Kate with the snorkeling equipment.

"Heck," Jared said, "I knew I forgot something. You want to try it again, Kate?"

Kate slicked back her hair and held up one palm in surrender. "Not your way, thanks. I think David will make a much better instructor."

"This is your lucky day, Kate. You get both of us." Jared unfastened his jeans to reveal a pair of swimming briefs. He waded toward shore and tugged off the wet denim and his soaked shirt while David helped Kate put on the mask.

Jared took over the instruction when he returned, giving orders in a crisp, efficient manner.

A few minutes later, all three of them were swimming toward the reefs. Jared and David kept Kate between them as they guided her through the underwater wonderland.

Kate forgot all about Jared's teasing revenge as she came face-to-face with one spectacular fish after another. The colors were glorious. Jeff Taylor had been right when he said swimming around the reefs was like swimming inside an aquarium. Each amazingly tame fish was more outrageously beautiful than the last.

The morning sun danced in the crystal clear water, creating a fabulous underwater garden of coral and sand. Kate lost track of time as first David and then Jared drew her attention to yet another beautiful scene. When Jared finally tugged her ankle and motioned her to surface, she did so with reluctance.

He raised his mask and grinned down at her delighted expression as they stood waist-deep in the water. "You like that, huh?"

"It's fantastic. I've never seen anything like it. Absolutely beautiful. You're so lucky to live in a place where you get to do this every day."

Jared eyed her for a moment and then nodded. "Dave and I like it, don't we?" He looked at his son, who was standing in shallower water.

"Yeah, it's great. But I like Disneyland, too. Dad took me there last year."

"I'll take this, even over Disneyland. Well, I thank you both for the lessons, though I will do the polite thing and refrain from commenting on the first step." Kate wrinkled her nose. "Do we have to stop now?"

Jared shook his head. "You two don't have to quit, but I've got work to do. Some of us are not on vacation. I'll see you both later. Dave, don't forget to take care of the equipment when you're done here."

"I won't, Dad. Come on, Ms Inskip. Let's go look at another section of coral."

"Sounds like a wonderful idea."

Kate lowered her mask and turned to follow the boy back under the water. She was aware of Jared standing in the shallows watching them for a few minutes, but when she surfaced a while later, he was gone.

The small, aching sensation of regret she felt startled her.

The invitation to dinner in Jared and David's private quarters arrived late the next afternoon. Kate had been lazing in the shade on her veranda, telling herself she ought to be doing something useful, such as plotting a new novel, when the knock sounded on her door. She got to her feet and went to answer the summons. A young man in the resort's livery of white slacks and a flowered shirt stood on the threshold. He was obviously having a hard time containing a grin.

"Message for you, Miss Inskip. From the management. I had special instructions to wait for a reply."

"Thanks." Kate glanced curiously at the childish print on the outside of the envelope. She unfolded the single sheet of lined binder paper and read the short, painstakingly lettered message.

"Please come to dinner tonight. We will have it at seven." It was signed David Hawthorne.

"Just a minute," Kate told the messenger. "I'll give you a reply."

She found a piece of stationery with the resort's crest on it and carefully wrote a short note of acceptance. Then she folded it, slipped it into an envelope and sent the courier off with it.

As soon as she closed the door behind the young man she went straight to her closet and examined her wardrobe. Sarah and Margaret had done an excellent job of packing. Kate smiled to herself as she made her selection.

At precisely seven o'clock that evening, dressed in a demure ankle-length sheath of polished green cotton and gold sandals, Kate walked down the path to the gracious, airy home where Jared and David lived.

The house was set a short distance from the resort. It was nestled in the lush island foliage on the top of a bluff and commanded a sweeping view of the cove and the small outlying shoals and islets that protected Amethyst Island.

Kate hesitated briefly before raising her hand to knock at the front door. She'd never accepted an invitation quite like this one before, and her curiosity was aroused. She wondered if Jared knew what his son had planned for the evening. Cautiously she tapped on the door. A moment later she heard pounding footsteps and then the door was flung open.

"Hi," David said. "I knew you'd come. Everything's ready. Dad's in the living room."

Kate stepped inside the cool foyer and glanced curiously at her surroundings. There was a subtle harmony to the bleached wood floors, the sisal matting and the graceful greenery. The front of the house seemed to be one vast open window that caught the breeze and the spectacular view.

David led the way toward a large room furnished in rattan. Kate followed her host down two steps and looked across the room to see Jared standing at a brass and glass beverage cart. He turned to glance at her as she walked slowly toward him. His gaze was appreciative and his smile was slow.

"I'm innocent," he said. "This was all David's idea."

"I believe you." Kate smiled at the boy, who was looking enormously pleased with himself.

David looked at his father. "Come on, Dad, you're supposed to pour her a drink. Then I'll introduce her to Jolly."

"Thank you for reminding me, Dave. What will you have, Kate?"

"A little sherry will be fine."

Jared nodded and picked up a bottle. "When is the restaurant kitchen sending dinner over, son?"

"I told them to send it at seven-thirty. Is that okay?" David looked momentarily anxious.

"That sounds fine." Jared handed the glass of sherry to Kate, his gaze a mixture of amusement and sensual intensity. "Dave tells me he has arranged everything this evening."

David nodded in satisfaction. "Come on, Kate. I want you to meet Jolly."

"Who's Jolly?" Kate obediently followed the boy out of the living room and into a spacious kitchen. A large green-and-yellow bird crouched malevolently on top of a black wrought-iron cage. "Oh, I see. He doesn't look especially Jolly."

"Jolly is short for Jolly Roger," Jared explained.

Kate laughed. "Now that fits. Will he take off my finger if I try to scratch his head?"

"Of course not," David said.

"Wanna bet?" asked Jolly. But he stretched his neck out demandingly.

Kate scratched cautiously. "He's beautiful. Does he talk a lot?"

"You've just heard his entire vocabulary," Jared said.

"Wanna bet?" Jolly turned an annoyed eye on Jared.

"Fortunately," Jared said, "the two words he knows are very useful here on Amethyst."

Kate glanced around the kitchen and saw a number of pencil drawings tacked up on the refrigerator. She went for a closer look and discovered they were astonishingly charming sketches of the cove and the resort. "These are wonderful. Did you do them, Dave?"

"Yeah. You really like 'em?"

"Very much. You have a lot of talent."

David blushed happily. "Thanks. Well." He looked from one adult to the other and started to back out of the room. "Guess everything's under control, so I'd better be going."

Kate looked at him in surprise. "Aren't you staying for dinner?"

David shook his head quickly. "Carl Shimazu invited me to spend the night at his house. His mom said it was okay. Carl and I are going to study together." He looked at his father. "You don't have to worry about anything, Dad. I told the kitchen staff to take care of everything."

"Thanks, son." Jared's mouth quirked. "I appreciate that."

"Sure. Well, good night. See you guys later." With one last look around, David turned and bounded into the hall. A moment later the front door closed behind him.

Jared swirled the whiskey in his glass and led the way back into the living room. "What can I say? He means well. He likes you."

"I like him, too."

Kate wandered over to the expanse of open wall and took a deep breath of the fragrant night air. An odd nervousness was settling on her now that she was alone with Jared. When she had accepted the invitation she had been certain David would be around to act as a buffer. Instead, she was on her own.

The nervousness alarmed her. This was not like her at all. The only other time she could remember feeling nervous around a man in recent years was the time she had been stopped by a grim-looking motorcycle cop. She had been sure she was going to get a ticket. In the end she had given him an autographed book for his wife, instead. He'd been thrilled.

Jared came up behind her, not touching her. "The other night in the garden I got the impression you liked me, also. Did I get the signals mixed?"

"You're very direct, aren't you?"

"I don't have time to string this out, but even if I did, I probably wouldn't. You're right. I am a direct man, Kate. I don't like games."

"Your friend Letty says we strike sparks off each other."

"I guess we do. Is that so bad?"

Kate shook her head. "No, but I'm not sure it's good, either. Sparks can be dangerous."

"They can set fires," Jared agreed. "But I'll be honest with you, Kate. I've never had any woman set quite this kind of fire in me. I'm not sure exactly how to handle things, but I know I can't walk away and pretend this never happened. Can you?"

There was silence for a long moment. Then Kate said softly, "I told you I wasn't interested in a vacation fling."

"Is that why you disappeared so fast after the masquerade ball? You just aren't interested? I don't believe that."

She tilted her head thoughtfully to one side. "You want the truth? I got cold feet."

"I thought that might be it. At least you're honest about it."

"I also decided you were taking a lot for granted on the basis of a few kisses."

"And you wanted to put me in my place?"

Her fingers tightened on the glass. "No, not exactly. I just decided things were happening too quickly."

"If things don't happen quickly between us, they won't happen at all. Within a month you'll be gone."

"Yes." She moved uneasily, stepping away from him and turning to smile coolly. "Which is the best reason of all for not getting involved, isn't it? What's for dinner?"

"I don't know." Jared's mouth curved faintly. "David ordered everything. One of the side benefits of raising a kid around a resort is that he gets very sophisticated about such things as ordering up room service."

"I see. David does this for you a lot, then?"

"For your information, this is the first time he's ever tried his hand at matchmaking."

Kate winced. "Sorry, didn't mean to annoy you."

"Didn't you? I think you enjoy annoying me, Kate."

"Careful, you're getting paranoid."

"I'm not so sure about that. Sometimes I almost have the feeling I'm being tested in some way."

Kate's eyes widened in astonishment. "Good grief, what a weird thing to say. You really are paranoid." But she sensed some blundering masculine insight in his accusation and wondered silently what was happening to her.

Jared smiled again and held up his palm. "You're probably right. Let's call a truce, okay? The food will be here any minute and I'm hungry."

"So am I. I did some more snorkeling this morning and it gave me an appetite."

He eyed her warily. "About the snorkeling lesson yesterday. Can I assume you're not holding a grudge?"

"Just because you faked that fall and then dropped

me into the sea? Heavens, no. Why would I hold a grudge over a little thing like that?"

"Beats me. It wasn't as if I didn't have grounds for revenge or anything. But some women aren't as fair-minded as you are. David took pains to point out to me what a good sport you were about the whole thing."

Kate laughed softly, beginning to relax. "All right, I'll admit you might have had grounds for revenge. I shouldn't have ducked out the night of the masquerade without saying anything. I should have told you I'd changed my mind."

Jared grinned. "That's probably as close to an apology as I'll get, so I'll take it and be satisfied." He started to say something else and then paused as a knock sounded on the front door. "Ah, there's dinner. Let's see how creative the kid is."

David, with the help of the resort's restaurant staff, had outdone himself. The Brie-and-sun-dried-tomatoes appetizer was followed by impeccably fresh fish cooked in parchment and a beautifully arranged plate of exotic tiny sautéed vegetables. It was all lavishly served by a waiter who couldn't seem to hide his delight as he went about his duties. It was obvious the staff was enjoying the entire event.

When the excellent Chardonnay had been served, the linen napkins unfolded and the candles lit, the waiter bowed himself out the front door. Jared waited until he was gone, then he lounged back in his chair and looked across the table at Kate.

"You realize, of course, that this will be all over the resort by midnight, if it isn't already?"

"Uh-huh."

"Certain assumptions concerning our relationship will be made."

"Probably."

"Just thought I'd warn you." Jared nodded once and raised his wineglass. "Here's to us and the month we have. Let's not waste it, Kate."

Kate felt her insides tighten, but at the same time a thrill of anticipation was soaring through her. She looked into Jared's silvery eyes as she obediently raised her own glass and the poignant sense of familiarity nearly overwhelmed her. "To us," she whispered.

"Why don't you tell me how you go about writing a book?" Jared suggested when the toast was finished.

"All right. If you'll tell me how you go about running a resort."

"It's a deal."

To Kate's surprise, it was suddenly easy to talk to him. The conversation flowed so effortlessly now. She felt lighter than air, caught up once more in that dangerously seductive certainty that she knew Jared far more intimately than could possibly have been the case.

When they had polished off the white-chocolate-and-macadamia-nut dessert, Jared got to his feet. He reached down to grasp Kate's wrist and drew her up beside him. "Come on, I want to show you something."

"Not your etchings, I hope."

"I think you're going to find this a lot more interesting than etchings. And I want you to remember I thought of this angle all on my own. David didn't have anything to do with it."

"Where are we going?" Kate asked as he led her down the hall.

"To my study."

Not his bedroom. Kate wondered at the sense of wistful disappointment she felt.

When Jared opened the door into a book-lined room, she stepped inside and gazed around with deep interest. "Very nice."

He released her wrist and went over to a glass-fronted cabinet that housed several very old leather-bound volumes. On one of the shelves was the black dagger Jared had been wearing the previous evening.

"What are those?" Kate's attention was instantly captured by the sight of the old books.

"Some journals, business papers and a ship's log belonging to Roger Hawthorne plus a diary that his wife, Amelia, kept."

Kate's eyes widened in astounded delight. "Are you serious?" She flew across the room to stand in front of the cabinet. She stared longingly down at the aging volumes.

"Take a look." Jared opened the glass doors, smiling with satisfaction as Kate reached carefully inside for one of the journals.

She stroked the cracked leather cover lovingly. "Do you realize what you have here? A pirate's personal journals. What an incredible thought. And the diary of the bride he kidnapped. I would sell my soul for these volumes."

"I wasn't planning to ask such a high price, but if you insist, I won't turn you down."

Her head came up swiftly as she sensed the sensual meaning in his softly spoken words. The expression in his eyes made her catch her breath, and she forgot about the treasure she held in her hands.

"Jared?"

"You can examine the journals any time you like while you're here on Amethyst."

"Thank you." She was breathless. The heat in his gaze was warming her from the inside out, "Thank you very much." Kate put the old volume carefully back into the glass cabinet and stood very still.

After a long, shuddering moment of silence, Jared reached out to touch her cheek. "Whatever else it will be, Kate, it won't be just a fling. You know that, don't you?"

She felt his fingers tremble slightly on her skin. When he dropped his hand, she was trapped by the molten silver of his eyes. Surely she had known this man all her life. "Yes," she said. "I know."

He picked up a blanket that lay folded on the end of the sofa, took Kate's hand again and led her out of the study onto the shadowy veranda that overlooked the sea.

FIVE

The night was heavy and warm. Kate fell silent as Jared led her out into the darkness. She was back under the same spell that had captured her the night of the masquerade ball, she realized. But tonight there would be no escape. Jared's hand wrapped hers in a strong, sure grip, and she had no desire to be freed.

Without an explanation he tugged her down the steps of the veranda to a path that led toward the water. They walked through a grove of shadowy palms and out into a small, secluded moonlit cove. This was not Crystal Cove, the main hotel beach, but a private, hidden place that Kate sensed was not open to the public. Wavelets foamed softly on the shore, glistening in the pale light.

"Where are you taking me?" she asked, not particularly concerned with the answer.

"To a special place I know. And, no, before you ask, I don't take a lot of female guests there."

"I wasn't going to ask."

"Starting to trust me?"

"I just don't feel like asking too many questions to-night," she said.

His hand tightened around hers. "Good. It's probably better that way."

At the edge of the sand they stopped and took off their shoes. Then they walked to the end of the beach. There Jared drew Kate into the shadows of a palm. He spread the blanket on the ground and stood looking at her, his face taut with controlled hunger. When he made no further move, Kate knew he was waiting for her to make the final decision.

She hesitated a moment and then walked into his arms. They closed around her, safe, strong and wonderfully familiar, wonderfully right.

"Promise me you won't regret this in the morning," Jared said into her ear, his fingers tangling in her hair. "I want this to be right for both of us. No recriminations, no reprisals, no apologies."

"I wouldn't have come this far with you if I had any more doubts."

"The other night I thought you knew what you wanted, but you still left without a word."

"I told you, the other night there were other complications. Things were happening too fast. Nothing felt real. Then I realized your friend Letty was matchmaking and I really got nervous. I needed time to think."

"No more thinking. I've tried to think this through for the past couple of days. It got me nowhere." Jared groaned and pulled her close. Kate's body reacted instinctively to the hard, demanding male strength in him. His kiss was a heavy, drugging caress that intoxicated her with emotion and sensual excitement. His mouth moved on hers as his hands moved on her body—slowly, intimately, hungrily.

Kate felt the zipper of her sheath slide down the length of her spine to her waist, and the dress crumpled to her hips. Her small, lacy bra fell away under his touch. Jared leaned his forehead against hers and looked down at her breasts.

"I knew you would be this lovely. I want you so much. I haven't been able to think of anything else since I saw you in that alley on Ruby." He touched her nipples, sliding his thumbs across them slowly until they flowered into firm peaks. "You make me ache in a way I haven't ached in a very long time."

She trembled under the warm honey of his words. "I have never ached this way." The honesty in her own words amazed her. She hadn't meant to say them, but now that they were said it was all right. It was the truth.

"Letty was right about us striking sparks off each other. But some of the sparks are very, very exciting."

"Yes." Kate slowly unbuttoned his shirt until it hung open and then she pushed it off entirely. The garment fell to the sand, and she stroked Jared's sleek shoulders, loving the feel of the strong, muscled flesh.

Jared finished undressing her carefully, his hands gliding down over her hips, taking the dress and her panties with them. Then he was stroking her bare, rounded buttocks, cupping her and lifting her up against him. She felt rough denim and the cold metal fastening of his jeans against her stomach. The heaviness of his manhood thrust against the fabric. The fullness of his arousal was almost shocking.

"You feel so good," Jared whispered as he eased her down onto her back on the blanket. He knelt beside her and stroked the length of her bare leg. "Warm and soft and sexy."

"Not prickly?"

"Not prickly at all." He bent his head and kissed the hollow of her stomach. "I should have guessed all the prickliness was designed to protect something very special."

Unable to help herself, Kate arched sensuously under his touch, closing her eyes and moaning softly. Her fingers tightened on his shoulders and she urged him closer. He was hard all over, the contours of his back defining his physical strength.

Jared came down on top of her, his bare chest crushing her gently. So much crisp, dark hair on that chest, Kate thought.

He was still wearing his jeans, and Kate found the texture of the cloth against her naked leg strangely exciting. It became almost unbearably so when Jared slid down the length of her. His mouth was all over, tasting her, exploring her body, covering her with hot, damp kisses. She gasped and her head tipped back over his arm when she felt his teeth lightly graze her breast. Then she felt his tongue curl around her nipple and she laughed in soft delight, lightheaded with the thrill of it all.

When he moved lower still, she thought she would fly apart into a million glittering pieces.

"Jared."

"I'm not going anywhere. You taste like the sea."

"I can't stand...Jared, wait. Come here. Please." She coiled one leg around his thigh and tightened her grip on him, pulling him upward again. Her hands slid down his back. "Your jeans."

"I know. I'll get rid of them." He rolled to one side, unfastened his denims and slid out of the last of his clothing. He paused long enough to draw a small packet from one pocket, fumbled with it for a few seconds and then he came back to her in a hot, enveloping rush.

"This is so perfect," Kate said, looking up at him through half-closed lashes. His body was lean, hard and beautifully male. "Maybe too perfect." The strength in him was controlled and all the more powerful because of that control. "You're so perfect."

His smile was slow and deeply sensual as he bent over her. "Remember that in the morning. Promise?"

"I promise."

He caught his breath as he put his heavy thigh over one of her twisting, restless legs, pinning her gently. "Now put your arms around me and open yourself for me. I want you more than I can ever remember wanting anything in my life."

"I want you, too." She was stunned at the depths of her own need. Such incredible passion would have a high price. Nothing came free in this world. She looked up at Jared, studying his shadowed face.

"I'm glad you want me. I need you to want me. Lord, how I need it," he said fiercely. His expression was stark in the moonlight; the desire in him unmistakable. His eyes glittered with it. The hand that covered her stomach shook with it.

Jared slid his warm palm down to the soft hair above her thighs. Kate parted her legs for him, lifting herself helplessly against his hand. She felt his fingers slip down into her softness and search out the growing dampness between her legs. Slowly he explored her secrets with roughened fingers, coaxing more of the liquid heat from her until she could not think of anything except the mind-spinning passion. He kissed her, filling her mouth and then withdrawing in a tantalizing rhythm that set up the more intimate pattern that would soon follow.

When Jared moved at last, settling himself deliberately between her legs, Kate cried out and sank her nails into his shoulders.

"Yes, sweetheart. Show me how much you want me." He pushed himself slowly, relentlessly into her heat. "So good," he muttered hoarsely. "So tight and hot and sweet. I'm going to lose my mind."

She clung to him, wrapping herself around him as he filled her completely and then he began to move, pulling almost free of her, hesitating and then driving as deeply into her softness as he could.

Over and over, Jared repeated the excruciatingly exciting rhythm until Kate was lost in her need. She could no longer think clearly or question or talk. She could only feel, and what she felt was unlike anything she had ever known in her life. She was on fire with passion, a white-hot banner of searing flame that threatened to consume her. It would have been terrifying if it hadn't been so totally irresistible; so totally right.

Together they twisted and writhed on the blanket, clutching each other as if locked in mortal combat. They rolled over and over, fighting for the release that was racing toward them out of the darkness.

As the sensual battle moved toward its inevitable conclusion, Kate experienced a wild, surging sense of freedom and exhilaration that was beyond anything she had ever known in her life. She cried out with it.

"Jared."

"Now," he muttered against her throat as he pushed her onto her back. He grabbed her wrists and anchored them above her head, muttering hot, encouraging words into her ear as he held her. "Let it go. Give it to me. All of it. *All of it.*" His muscles bunched and his back arched. "I've waited so long for you, sweetheart. Too long."

Pinned beneath him, Kate opened her eyes just enough to see that Jared's face was set in a rigid mask of emotion. She didn't think he even knew what he was saying. His words were thick and hoarse, almost anguished. He surged deeply into her one last, shattering time and she was spun outward into the shimmering sea.

And suddenly she knew without a shadow of a doubt where she had seen him before. He was the man in her dreams, the one she had first begun to know when she had changed from girl into woman; the one who had haunted her all these years; the one she put into every book she wrote. This was her pirate—fierce, tender, passionate and proud.

The shock of recognition merged with the sensual storm that was sweeping through her and blotted out everything from Kate's mind. She cried out and then she was lost.

Reality trickled back slowly, mixing with moonlight and the soft sounds of the sea. Kate was aware of Jared's arm across her breasts and of the dampness of his warm skin. He was sprawled beside her, one leg still flung over her thighs, his chin just touching her head. He was heavy, but his weight made her feel protected and safe.

She remembered the fleeting instant of recognition a few minutes earlier and shuddered.

"Cold?" Jared stirred lazily, turning onto his back, one hand behind his head. He looked up at her with eyes that gleamed with the banked embers of a fire that had been only temporarily quenched.

"No." She touched his moonlit-etched face with curious fingers.

"What's wrong?" He kissed her fingertips as they traced his mouth.

"Nothing's wrong. It's just that I've had this odd feeling I know you."

"You do know me. In fact, I'd say that you know me very well now."

She crossed her elbows on his chest and studied him. "Better than you think."

He laughed, his voice husky and replete with satisfaction. "Is that a warning?"

She shrugged. "Maybe."

"I'll keep it in mind." He stroked her bare shoulder. "You know something? You're not prickly at all when you're in this mood."

"I'm glad you approve."

"I approve, all right. I can see the trick will be to keep you in the right frame of mind as much of the time as possible."

"That could take a lot of work on your part."

"I'll devote every spare minute to the job." Jared snagged his fingers in her hair, pulled her mouth down to his and kissed her hard. "Damn, but you're a delight. You make me feel like a million bucks. Two million."

"I feel pretty good myself."

"What piece of good luck brought you to my island, sweet Kate?"

"The combined effects of overwork and two well-intentioned, interfering friends. Left to my own devices, I would never have made it as far as Amethyst Island. I'd still be sitting at home, staring at a computer screen."

Jared framed her face with his hands, his expression turning serious. "What's your home like? A snazzy little apartment in Seattle?"

"I like it."

"How long have you lived there?"

"Since my husband went off to devote himself to his talent."

"What was he like, this ex-husband of yours?"

"He's a man who has the soul of a poet. A writer of great undiscovered literary potential, or so he told me."

"Why did you marry him?"

"Good question. When we were first introduced we were both aspiring writers. I thought he was sensitive, intelligent and supportive," Kate said slowly. "And he was. At first. He liked the fact that I had a full-time job and could support him while he devoted himself to his writing. But then I got published and he didn't, and he blamed me for his failure and things went downhill from there. I now realize, of course, that he was really weak, neurotic, self-centered and a whiner. Goes to show how one can change one's opinion of a person, doesn't it?"

"Where is he now?"

"I'm not sure. Last I heard he was hanging out at an elite writers' colony, reading his poems to other writers who all agree with him that the only reason they're unpublished is because the world does not appreciate true genius."

"Miss him?"

"No." Kate smiled. "And I know he doesn't miss me. Toward the end of our relationship, I had gotten tired of coddling his overinflated ego and even more tired of dealing with his nasty little remarks about my writing. I'm afraid I turned a tad shrewish."

"I'm shocked. You? A shrew?"

"That was how Harry saw me."

"Probably because he didn't know how to deal with you," Jared said easily. "So your ex turned tail and ran, hmm?"

"Packed his bags and walked out after making a suitably dramatic farewell speech. I cried for about fifteen minutes, and then my friends Sarah and Margaret came over and took me out for champagne and pizza. They told me I was lucky to see the last of good old Harry, and within forty-eight hours I knew they were right. But it took a while to put it all behind me."

Jared nodded soberly. "Harry was not the man for you."

"Truer words were never spoken." The man for her existed only between the covers of her books and here on Amethyst Island, Kate reflected silently.

Jared grinned. "On the other hand, be sure you remember what you yourself said earlier."

"What's that?"

"Unlike your ex-husband, I am perfect. Your very words."

She laughed softly. "I'm not sure you can hold me responsible for that remark. I was under the influence of a lot of raging hormones at the time."

"If that's the way you're going to be about it, I'll just have to enrage your hormones until you say it again." Jared shifted, rolling her beneath him. "And again and again."

"We could be here all night."

"That thought had occurred to me." He lowered his head and took her mouth.

A long time later Kate sighed and snuggled close. "Perfect," she murmured.

The next few days passed in a haze of passion and laughter. Kate went snorkeling in the cove with David, toured the island with Jared and his son in a Jeep, ate papaya and impossibly fresh fish and spent every possible stolen hour in the arms of her dream lover.

Those hours had to be grabbed when they were available because Jared, Kate soon learned, in addition to being a father, was a very busy man. His schedule was unpredictable and usually very full. One moment he was going over special banquet arrangements with his food and beverage manager and the next he was dealing with a crisis involving the pool filter machinery. Kate sought him out one afternoon and discovered him helping his staff fold a huge stack of towels in the resort's hot laundry room.

"The assistant housekeeper's daughter is having her baby. She went over to Ruby to be with her and two of the laundry room staff went along. They're all family. None of them made it back this morning, so we're short-handed," he'd explained tersely, folding a towel with precision.

"Want me to give you a hand?" Kate asked, picking up a fluffy white towel that bore the Crystal Cove crest.

Jared blinked in surprise and then grinned broadly. "I'll take any help I can get."

"Just be sure you also take a few bucks off my room bill for today, okay?"

"You bet. Want to flip a coin for the day's tab? Double or nothing?"

"Not on your life, Hawthorne. Unlike everyone else around here, I only bet on a sure thing."

The housekeeping staff had found the exchange hilarious, and the story was soon all over the resort. Afterward Kate found extra towels every day in her room.

Jared made no secret of their liaison and Kate soon realized that everyone, from the resort staff to David, Letty and the colonel, was delighted with the way events were unfolding.

It should have been a perfect island affair, and Kate told herself it would have been if it weren't for two things. The first was that the end was preordained. She was, after all, holding a return ticket to the States. Whenever she allowed herself to dwell on that fact, she got restless and depressed and had to consciously push aside the emotions.

The second factor that stood in the way of her total enjoyment of the affair with Jared Hawthorne was a little harder to pin down, but it filled her with increasing unease. It had to do with the fact that she had seen him make another midnight trek to the Hawthorne castle with Max Butterfield and she had begun to realize she did not particularly care for Max. His incessant references to the great novel he had not yet written reminded her too much of her ex-husband.

On the night Jared and Max made the second trip to the castle, Jared had taken Kate back to her room right after dinner in the hotel dining room. He had made hot, urgent love to her and then told her he had to go home early because the baby-sitter couldn't stay with David past midnight.

Something had not rung true. She had known Max was back on the island, however, after being away for a few days. Kate had lain awake for a long time after Jared had left, questions and doubts and pure curiosity tumbling about in her brain. Then, drawn by a premonition, she had dressed in jeans and a dark shirt and walked down the path through the jungle to the point where it branched off to the castle.

She had stood concealed in the shadows for a long time before she had heard Max's complaining voice and the sound of his labored breathing. A moment later the fat man and Jared had passed her on their way to the castle.

Kate had waited a long time for them to return, but finally had given up and gone back to her own room. She did not get much sleep that night.

No matter how she looked at it, Jared had lied to her. He had not hurried home to his son.

The next morning, Kate sat in a lounger on a terrace overlooking the cove and wondered what to do next. Over and over again she toyed with the idea of confronting Jared and asking him what was going on, but she always backed off from that approach when she remembered that he had deliberately misled her. It was obvious he did not want her to know what he was doing with Max Butterfield. If she confronted him, he would probably lie to her, and she didn't want to hear his lies.

She had to face the knowledge that, though Jared might appear to have stepped straight out of her fantasies, the truth was, she knew very little about him.

"Good morning," sang out a familiar, cheerful voice. "How's the antistress campaign going?"

Kate shook off her somber mood and smiled at Letty Platt. "Terrific. I feel like a new woman. And I've got some fascinating reading." She indicated the diary of Amelia Cavendish that lay in her lap.

Letty glanced at the leather-bound volume. "So Jared has let you actually touch his precious old Hawthorne journals, I see. Congratulations. He's very protective of those books. Keeps them in a locked glass case."

"I know and I don't blame him. They're fascinating, once you decipher the handwriting. They're in amazingly good condition, too. But that's because the paper used in the old days was of such fine quality, not like the cheap, disposable stuff we use now."

Letty nodded, sitting down on a nearby lounger. "Discover anything interesting about our founding father?"

"This is Amelia's diary, not Roger's, and yes, I'm finding out a lot of interesting tidbits. For example, did you know that she had been in love with Roger Hawthorne since she was a young girl?"

"Really? I thought he just happened to spot her when he went back to England looking for a bride."

"Nope. She was the daughter of the lord who owned the estates that bordered his father's lands and she'd had a crush on him for years. He was well aware of it, the cad. Used to tease her unmercifully. But he also danced with her when she made her come out in London. He kissed her that night. Listen to this, Letty."

I was transported the moment his lips touched mine. I did not dream such unbearable joy existed. I know I should not have allowed him such liberties, but I vow I was helpless to resist him. It seems I have loved Roger forever, and at long last he is discovering he loves me. Surely he loves me. He is too much the gentleman to have kissed me otherwise. I am in heaven as of this moment. I cannot wait until he makes an offer for me.

"Uh-oh," Letty said. "Let me guess what happened next. The rogue left England and poor Amelia never got her offer."

"Afraid not. Hawthorne didn't actually seduce her, but he certainly got passionate on a number of occasions and led her to believe he was going to ask for her hand in marriage. Then, without any warning, he ups and leaves the country without a word of explanation and doesn't return for three years. Amelia was devastated. Cried inconsolably for days."

"Poor girl."

"She turned out to be the feisty type, though. When she finally recovered from her heartbreak she was determined never to give her heart to another man. She scorned all offers of marriage, though her family pleaded and threatened when she turned down one eligible male after another."

"She'd really had it with men, hmm? Can't say that I blame her. Why did Roger Hawthorne leave England so suddenly?"

"I don't know yet. Amelia just says he split without bothering to say goodbye. He was a second son and so couldn't inherit. I expect he decided to go off and make his fortune as a pirate, and the thought that poor Amelia would get her heart broken didn't occur to him."

"Or didn't bother him too much if it did occur to him. Typical male in many respects."

"I'm at the part now where he's just returned. Amelia has found out he's in London and that he's asked her father for her hand in marriage. Apparently he's quite wealthy now and society is willing to overlook the little matter of how he got so rich. Amelia writes that her parents are delighted with the offer. But she refuses to even see him. Says she is not about to trust him with her heart a second time. Can't wait to see what happens next."

"Well, we can guess, given the fact that the legend says he eventually kidnapped her and brought her back here."

Kate closed the book. "Something tells me she put up a good fight. She's really furious with him at this point."

"Maybe her relationship with Roger went the same way your relationship with Jared is going. I must tell you, Kate, we are all having a great time watching you two."

"I can tell. I feel as if I'm conducting a relationship inside a goldfish bowl."

"You don't know how good it is to see Jared getting involved emotionally at long last. He's been alone with only David for too many years. He needs a wife."

Kate stirred uneasily. "Come on, Letty. You know as well as I do that the kind of thing Jared and I have is probably going to end the day I catch my plane home."

Letty smiled complacently. "If Jared takes after Roger Hawthorne as much as I think he does, he won't let you get on that plane."

"He can't stop me," Kate said automatically.

Letty chuckled without opening her eyes. "Don't be ridiculous. Jared all but owns this island. He can do anything he wants around here. Just ask anyone."

Kate thought about Jared's midnight treks to the Hawthorne castle and went cold. What if Letty was right, she wondered. What if Jared really did run this island as if it were his own personal kingdom? What if the power he wielded around here had gone to his head and he had gotten involved in something dangerous or outside the law?

Her imagination was running wild, she told herself. "Letty, what do you know about Max Butterfield?"

"Max?" Letty opened one eye. "Not a lot. But then there isn't a lot to know. He's been out here forever.

He's the kind of guy who imagines himself to be another Hemingway and does a good enough job with the booze, but not an equally good job with the writing. Why? Did old Max make a pass?"

"No. I was just curious." She was about to ask another question when Jared's voice interrupted.

"There you are, Kate." He walked up behind Kate and leaned down to drop a hard, possessive kiss on her forehead. "I've been looking for you. Hi, Letty, how's it going?"

"Just fine, Jared. Kate has been filling me in on all the details from Amelia Cavendish's diary. It's about time someone read it cover to cover."

"I tried once, but I didn't get far. Pretty dull going. Roger's journals and log are a lot more interesting." Jared dropped lightly down onto the foot of Kate's lounger. "Who wants to read a woman's diary?" he added plaintively.

Kate punched him lightly in the ribs. "I'm having a great time reading it, I'll have you know. It's a heck of a lot more interesting than a ship's log."

"Ouch." Jared gave her a reproachful look as he massaged his injured ribs. "That's a fine way to treat a man who's just come out to invite you to a nice home-cooked dinner."

"Has David lined up the restaurant staff for us again?"

"Uh, no, not exactly."

Kate's brows rose as she saw the speculative gleam in Jared's eyes. "Really? Who's going to do the cooking? You and David?"

"As a matter of fact, we planned to let you do it."
Jared gave her his best buccaneer's smile. "Dave
hasn't had a home-cooked meal in ages. Neither have
I."

Letty gave a muffled laugh from her lounger. "Be
careful, Kate. Sounds like they're planning to take advantage of you."

"I'm supposed to be on vacation," Kate pointed out
loftily.

"Yeah, well, if you can't cook, just say so. Dave and
I will understand. It's not too late to order dinner
from the restaurant."

"I can cook," Kate retorted, feeling challenged.

"Are you sure?" Jared looked doubtful.

"Of course I'm sure," she snapped, thoroughly irritated now by his skeptical expression.

"It's okay to admit it if you can't. I mean, this being
the late twentieth century and all, there are probably
a lot of women who never really learned to cook.
They've got their careers and stuff to think of first, I
guess and..."

"I told you, I can cook."

"Well, if you really think you can handle it..."

"I can handle it."

"You're sure it's not too much trouble?"

"It's not too much trouble, dammit. Haven't you
got some work you should be doing?"

"Yeah." Jared got to his feet and leaned down for
another quick, satisfied kiss. "There's a major plumb-
ing disaster going on in the south wing. I'd better
check on the repairs. See you around six. You can

AN IMPORTANT MESSAGE FROM THE EDITORS

Dear Reader,

Because you've chosen to read one of our fine novels, we'd like to say "thank you"! And, as a **special** way to thank you, we've selected <u>two more</u> of the books you love so well, **and** a picture frame to send you absolutely _**FREE!**_

Please enjoy them with our compliments...

Editor,
The Best of the Best

P.S. And because we value our customers, we've attached something extra inside ...

EDITOR'S
FREE GIFT SEAL
THANK YOU

Peel off seal and
Place inside...

THE EDITOR'S "THANK YOU"
FREE GIFTS INCLUDE:

▶ Two "The Best of the Best" novels
▶ A lovely picture frame

PLACE
FREE GIFT
SEAL
HERE

YES! I have placed my Editor's "thank you" seal in the space provided above. Please send me 2 free books and a picture frame. I understand I am under no obligation to purchase any books, as explained on the back and on the opposite page.

183 MDL CF7N   (U-BB1-98)

_____   _____
NAME

_____
ADDRESS   APT. #

_____
CITY   STATE   ZIP

Thank you!

© 1995 MIRA BOOKS.   PRINTED IN THE U.S.A.

DETACH AND MAIL CARD TODAY.

THE BEST OF THE BEST™: HERE'S HOW IT WORKS

Accepting free books places you under no obligation to buy anything. You may keep the books and gift and return the shipping statement marked "cancel". If you do not cancel, about a month later we will send you 3 additional novels, and bill you just $4.24 each plus 25¢ delivery per book and applicable sales tax, if any.* That's the complete price — and compared to cover prices of $5.50 each — quite a bargain! You may cancel at any time, but if you choose to continue, every month we'll send you 3 more books, which you may either purchase at the discount price...or return to us and cancel your subscription.

*Terms and prices subject to change without notice. Sales tax applicable in N.Y.

pick up any supplies you need at Chan's grocery in town. Letty will show you the place. Tell Chan I sent you and he'll give you the resort discount."

Jared sauntered off, whistling.

Kate stared after him. "Correct me if I'm wrong, Letty, but did I just let myself get bamboozled into cooking a free meal for Jared and Dave?"

"That's what it sounded like to me." Letty looked over at her curiously. "Can you cook?"

"You're looking at the best pizza maker this side of Seattle."

"Pizza!" Letty looked first astounded and then delighted. "If David isn't already half in love with you, he will be after tonight. Since Gabriella died, that boy's been eating restaurant food for just about every meal of the day except breakfast. When you stop and think about it, you realize he's been practically raised on such things as pâté-stuffed mushrooms and seafood curries. Not normal kid food at all."

The question was whether David's father would be as easily impressed, Kate decided. And if Jared did fall in love, would he admit it, either to her or himself?

The fact that she was even pondering such a question shocked Kate. It meant she had to face something she had been deliberately shying away from for the past few days. She was tumbling head over heels into love with the pirate of Amethyst Island.

SIX

The short trip into the tiny island town of Amethyst was a disturbing confirmation of everything Letty Platt had said about Jared's power on the island. Even more unnerving for Kate was the realization that even though this was the first time she had left the resort grounds, she was already a well-known figure, and not because of her reputation as an author, she soon discovered to her chagrin.

"Ms Inskip, it is indeed a pleasure to serve you." The beaming owner of the small grocery brushed aside his young assistant who appeared to be his son and handled the transaction personally. "Allow me to give you the usual resort discount," he insisted as he bagged Kate's purchases.

"I think I can handle the regular prices." Kate reached for her purse.

"No, no, no. Impossible. I will not hear of it. Jared Hawthorne does a great deal of business with my small shop and the discount I give him is my way of thanking him. You understand?"

"Yes, of course, but these are my groceries, not Mr. Hawthorne's. I'm buying them for personal use, not for the resort."

"But you are a close personal friend of Jared's and I must insist you accept the discount."

"But I really don't want it or need it."

Letty stepped close and murmured, "I wouldn't argue with him if I were you, Kate. Mr. Chan will be hurt, Jared will be annoyed and you'll lose the battle, anyway. This is Jared's discount and you're entitled to it. Let it go at that."

Kate sighed. She knew it wasn't worth an argument. She summoned up a properly grateful smile. "Thank you, Mr. Chan. You're very kind."

"Not at all, not at all." He rang up the sale on a cash register that looked as though it had been around since before one of the less recent wars. "Please give my best to Jared."

Kate took the paper sack full of pizza fixings and turned to follow a grinning Letty out of the store. Several people glanced at her with open curiosity and big smiles.

"What, exactly, do you think Mr. Chan meant when he called me a close personal friend of Jared's?"

Letty shot her a slanting glance. "What do you think he meant?"

"I was afraid of that. Does everyone on the island know that I'm...that Jared and I have been that—" she cleared her throat "—that close?"

"Probably. Does it bother you?"

"It annoys me," Kate snapped as she dumped the

sack of groceries into the back of the small Jeep Letty was driving. "It's an invasion of personal privacy."

"If you wanted a lot of personal privacy," Letty said as she put the Jeep in gear, "you shouldn't have gotten involved in an affair with the biggest honcho on the island."

Kate closed her eyes in brief frustration. "You've got a point. Getting involved with Jared is probably not the brightest thing I've ever done. Maybe the tropical heat has warped my brain. Where are we going now?"

"Thought we'd make a quick stop at a dress shop run by a friend of mine. She carries some nice things, and her prices are a lot better than the ones in the resort's gift shop."

Kate perked up. "Sounds like a great idea."

But twenty minutes later when Kate selected a colorful full-length island dress and asked to have it hemmed, she was confronted with another example of Jared's inescapable presence. He might as well have been looking over her shoulder, she thought wryly.

"I'll have my seamstress hem it immediately," the shop owner promised. "It will be delivered to the resort this afternoon. Will that be soon enough?"

"There's no great rush," Kate said quickly. "I can pick it up tomorrow."

"I wouldn't hear of it." The woman waved the idea aside with a graceful movement of her hand. "You're a personal friend of Jared's, and I insist. It's the least I can do. After all, Jared was the one who loaned me the capital I needed to open this shop. I'm delighted to be able to do a favor for a friend of his. Heavens, just about everyone on the island is happy to extend a few favors to Jared. Isn't that right, Letty?"

"I'm afraid so." Letty's eyes brimmed with amusement. "Come on, Kate. Let's take a peek inside the gallery next door. You might see something you like."

"And get it at a Hawthorne discount?" Kate asked dryly.

"Probably. Mary Farrell, who runs it, gets most of her business from the resort visitors. She undoubtedly feels she owes Jared a favor, too. Her artists would all be starving if it weren't for the customers Crystal Cove sends her way."

Kate threw up her hands. "I give up. Why don't you all just admit you're living in a feudal kingdom and buy Jared a crown?"

"Not exactly a feudal kingdom," Letty said, laughing. "Just a very small town on a very small island that's tucked away in a very far-off corner of the world. If it weren't for Jared Hawthorne and his resort, Amethyst would either be completely deserted or look a lot more like Port Ruby, a run-down, sleazy dump. People around here know that."

"And they're suitably grateful."

"You could say that."

"You know something, Letty? I'll bet things around here worked very much the same way back when Roger Hawthorne was in charge."

"I wouldn't be surprised."

* * *

Kate came to a halt on the path, glanced quickly back over her shoulder and then ducked under the heavy chain that guarded the route to the Hawthorne castle.

She felt extremely daring as she slipped past the barrier. She was now on forbidden territory.

There was no real reason to worry about being seen, though she continued to glance back over her shoulder. There was no reason to be nervous, either, she reminded herself. She had been at Crystal Cove long enough to learn the routine. It was barely dawn and no self-respecting guest at the resort arose at this hour. Neither did members of the staff, as far as Kate could discern. Life was definitely more relaxed on a South Seas island.

She would have the castle to herself, and that was exactly what she wanted. Her curiosity had become overwhelming.

Earlier in the week she had dutifully signed on for the official tour of the castle and had been bitterly disappointed. An enthusiastic guide had led the small group of interested guests along the winding path to the picturesque ruins, but no one had been allowed to do any in-depth exploring.

The young man had told everyone the story of Roger Hawthorne, a rather sanitized version compared to the edition Kate was reading in Amelia's diary.

The Hawthornes had lived on Amethyst Island for many years and had produced several children, despite Amelia's initial opposition to the marriage. That information had amused the small crowd. The family had eventually moved back to England when Roger's older brother had died without an heir, leaving the estates and a title to Roger.

The castle had remained empty ever since.

"And in such a dangerous state of disrepair that the resort management allows visitors only as far as the front hall at the present time," the guide had concluded. "Renovations are planned and someday soon large sections of the castle will be open for viewing."

But Kate had seen no sign of the renovations, nor any evidence of workmen around the place. She had, however, seen two sets of fresh footprints in the dust on a circular staircase at the back of the shadowy hall. Something told her the prints had been left by Jared and his large friend Max.

Kate had awakened this morning with the sure and certain knowledge that she could no longer contain her anxious curiosity. She had to know what was going on. Her intimate relationship with Jared made it impossible to ignore his mysterious comings and goings any longer.

The castle was supposed to be a crumbling ruin, forbidden to everyone, yet Jared had taken Max Butterfield up to it at midnight on at least two occasions, and the two men had apparently gone well beyond the front hall.

Kate was rapidly becoming convinced that whatever was going on at the castle at night was either illegal or dangerous or both. She had to know the truth.

It was a long hike along the narrow path to the Hawthorne castle. The route wound through the dense tropical growth above Crystal Cove and continued on for some distance through more heavy foliage until, with no warning, it ended abruptly in front of the old stone ruin.

Kate came to a halt and caught her breath while she studied the dark pile of stone in the dawn light.

The Hawthorne castle was more of a well-fortified stone house than a true castle, she decided. It was not a huge place, just a three-story structure pierced with narrow windows. There were no outer walls protecting a courtyard, gatehouses, moats or ramparts. There was, however, a tower that rose above the main building from which Roger Hawthorne had no doubt kept an eagle eye on the sea. From his aerie he could have watched for both opportunities and competitors.

The section of the castle that faced the sea was a solid wall of stone that merged with the dark lava that rose out of the waves. On the sea side, the castle was impregnable. The only approach was from the jungle side of the island.

During the tour, the guide had explained that Hawthorne and his crew had used the beach above Crystal Cove as a wharf. Cargoes had been unloaded, goods had been traded and business had been conducted on the spot where the resort now stood. The wealthy planters and others from nearby islands had been eager to buy whatever Hawthorne managed to get hold of and no one worried too much about the original owners of the goods.

Kate took a deep breath and walked cautiously through the massive stone entryway, following the path the tour guide had used the previous day. A moment later she found herself in the shadowy, high-ceilinged hall.

An eerie sensation rippled through her as she switched on her small flashlight. When she had stood in this room with a crowd full of curious resort guests, everything had seemed quite interesting. But this morning she felt as if she were standing in a room full of ghosts.

"Not exactly an English country house, Amelia," Kate whispered. "How did you stand it? I'll bet you were really annoyed when you realized you were supposed to set up housekeeping in this joint."

Kate walked across the floor to the circular stone staircase at the far end of the hall. The footprints were still there. She had not imagined them. The staircase went down, not up to the next level.

She leaned forward and splashed the light over the steps. They twisted and vanished into a forbidding darkness.

She had known the answers weren't going to come easily. She took a deep breath and considered her next move. There was no real option. If she wanted to know where the footsteps led, she would have to follow them.

When she started slowly down the narrow steps, she learned firsthand the meaning of having the hair on the back of her neck stand on end. Her fingers trembled as she grasped the flashlight. Her every instinct was alive with warning.

But she forced herself down the steps, following the muddled prints in the dust. It crossed her mind that the guide had emphasized several times that the castle was not structurally safe, but she decided that as long as she followed the footprints she would be reasonably safe. Jared and Max had come this way more than once, she reminded herself. And at midnight, too.

The gloom thickened around her as she descended below the level of the entry hall. Down here there were no slits in the walls to provide air and light. A dank, damp odor swirled around her. When she paused to flash the light around, Kate saw only more stone.

Then, without any warning, the stone steps came to an end in a tiny cell of a room. Perhaps this was a storage cellar, she thought. But when she examined the floor, she found that the footprints continued on, straight into a wall. There must be some sort of concealed doorway in the stone, she decided, but she had no idea of where to begin hunting for the hidden lock.

There were more prints leading off in the opposite direction back under the staircase. Kate followed these to a dark opening that proved to be a doorway. The door itself was long gone. When she flashed her light down the dank hall that was revealed, she saw a barred room that must have been used as a dungeon or secured storage room at one time.

Her uneasiness grew. The more she studied the barred room, the more it looked like a dungeon cell. Kate suddenly wanted very badly to get back upstairs into the light. She started quickly up the steps, stumbling in her haste.

When she was within sight of the last step, Kate switched off the flashlight and quickened her pace. She couldn't wait to get out into the warm light of the new day. Later, when she was safely back in her room, she would try to figure out what to do next. Perhaps she should confront Jared, after all. But what would she do if he simply denied everything? She could not bear the thought that he might be a real-life pirate.

The questions hammered at her, driving her forward until she practically leaped up the last step.

She was so intent on getting out of the hall that she didn't even see the man who stood concealed in the shadows at the top of the dark staircase. When his arm closed suddenly around her, snagging her and pulling her back against a solid male body, Kate opened her mouth on a terrified scream.

There was no scream: a large hand clamped over her mouth. Kate reacted in fear and rage, driving her elbow back into what felt like a very solid midsection. The blow brought a muffled curse, and for an instant the man's grip slackened.

That was all the time Kate needed. She moved, grasping his arm and stepping to one side in an effort to yank her assailant off balance. He went readily in the direction she wanted, too readily—the way Jared had that morning on the beach. Instead of losing his balance, he added so much force to the momentum she had established that Kate was thrown off her feet. In that instant Kate finally realized who she was dealing with.

"Jared."

He came down on top of her, pinning her to the floor. "Oh, Christ, it's you. I should have known. Quiet, you little fool. Sound carries. Are all romance writers so damnably curious?"

A new kind of anger surged through Kate. How dared he treat her like this? How dared he sneak around in the dark and grab unsuspecting people who were merely trying to get to the bottom of a few crucial questions?

"Let me go, you bastard. Let me go, dammit. You're a liar. A *liar*."

"Stop it," he ordered roughly. "Will you just stop struggling, for crying out loud? Listen to me, you little shrew. Settle down or you'll hurt yourself."

But Kate was too incensed to stop. She had never been so angry. She felt betrayed.

The battle was short and frantic, and Kate knew she had lost it before it had even begun. Nevertheless, she fought desperately, aware that she was overmatched. All two weeks' worth of self-defense lessons were discarded in a moment as she realized none of them would work. Instead she fought like a small, terrified creature that has become the prey of a much bigger, more dangerous predator.

She tried to kick out and found her leg anchored to

the floor by Jared's thigh. She tried to punch and got her wrists captured for her troubles. Jared did not hurt her, but he eventually succeeded in immobilizing her.

"That's enough," he said through his teeth. "You can't win, so stop wasting your energy."

A few minutes later, exhausted by her struggles, Kate followed his advice. She lay still, fighting to catch her breath. Her wrists were pinned on either side of her head in a parody of the way he had held her when he had made love to her. He was sprawled on top of her, using his weight to hold her still.

"That's better," he said after a minute's tense silence. He sat up slowly, releasing her carefully. His eyes never left her face. "Are you all right?"

"No." She sat up, aware that she was trembling with outrage. She brushed the dust from her shirt, concentrating on the small, useless task so that she would not have to meet his eyes. "I am not all right. How dare you manhandle me like this?"

He muttered something short and explicit under his breath as he got lithely to his feet. He reached down to haul her up beside him. His face was taut with anger.

"What the hell are you doing here?" Jared spoke through clenched teeth.

"What do you think I'm doing here? I came to take a closer look at the castle. The guided tour was a joke. We barely got to glance inside this hall. I wanted to see the rest of the place."

"You've been told the rest of the castle is off-limits."

"Yes, well, as you said, romance writers are a curious bunch."

Jared regarded her in silence for a few seconds. "Cut it out, Kate. I want the truth. Why are you here?"

"How did you know I was here?" she countered.

"I went by your room to see if you wanted to go for a dawn walk on the beach. It seemed so *romantic*. Thought it would appeal to you. You weren't there, so I figured you might have gone down to the cove on your own. You weren't there either, but the chain across the castle path was still swinging and I knew someone had come this way. When I walked into the hall I heard someone coming up the stairs."

"How very alert of you. I'm lucky you didn't break my neck."

"How was I to know it was you, dammit? I'm not in the mood for any of your sass, lady. I want some answers and I'm going to get them, but not here and not now."

"Why not here and now? I'd like a few answers, too."

"You've pushed your luck far enough today. The first thing we're going to do is get you back to the resort. I don't want you hanging around here any longer than necessary." He took hold of her arm and propelled her out of the hall and into the morning sunshine.

"Now, just one damned minute." Kate stumbled

and tried to pull free of his grip. Jared ignored her efforts. He dragged her swiftly along the path until they reached the chain that barred the way. There he paused long enough to push her underneath the metal links. He followed, ducking quickly beneath the barrier.

"All right," he said a moment later as they hit the main path back to the resort. "We're safe now. If anyone sees us here we can say we were down at the beach."

"Why do we have to make any explanations at all?" Kate cast him a furious glance.

"Because I said so."

"And whatever you say is law around here, is that it?"

"Now you're catching on."

He had hold of her hand now. To anyone else it would look like an affectionate grip, but Kate was thoroughly aware of the force behind it. She was relieved to be away from the castle ruins, but the wariness she felt around Jared was not making her feel much better. She began to think longingly of her cozy little apartment in Seattle.

"Where are we going?" she demanded as Jared walked her swiftly past her room and on toward the main resort building.

"My office. We can talk there without worrying about someone interrupting us."

She said nothing more as he led her through the empty lobby and down an open hallway to a room that overlooked the cove.

"In here." He closed the door behind them and pushed her toward a chair. "Sit down and talk." He went over to a side table and switched on a coffee machine.

"I think you're the one who should be doing the talking." Kate absently rubbed her wrist where he had gripped it. "What's going on at that castle, Jared? What are you and Max involved in?"

"Damn. You know about Max, too? You have been busy, haven't you?" He seemed totally wrapped up in watching the fresh coffee drip into the glass pot.

"I know you and Max have been paying some midnight visits to the castle." Kate decided she had nothing to lose at this point by admitting what she had seen.

"You're in this deeper than I realized. Who are you, Kate?"

The implied accusation infuriated her. "I'm exactly who I told you I am, a stressed-out writer on vacation. Nothing more and nothing less. Unlike you, I'm not living any lies."

"The weird part is that I believe you. I think I'd know if you were lying to me."

"I've got news for you—you're not the only one who can tell when someone is lying."

Jared sighed. "What made you start spying on Max and me? Research?"

"Hardly. I was coming back from the beach late my first night on the island and I decided to take a quick look at the castle. I had to hide in the bushes because you and Max were on the same path. When I spotted both of you going that way again a second time, I got curious."

"I'll just bet you did. Lord save all men from curious females."

Jared poured two cups of coffee and carried one over to her. When she took it without a word, he went around behind a massive carved desk and sat down.

"What's going on, Jared? What's the big secret?"

He sipped his coffee, looking very thoughtful. "To put it bluntly, my sweet, it's none of your damned business."

"Are you up to something illegal?"

"No."

"Then what's going on?" Kate was slightly relieved to hear the denial, but she was still thoroughly exasperated.

"It's nothing that concerns you, Kate. Furthermore, I'm ordering you to stay out of it."

"I don't take orders from you. If it's nothing illegal, then you won't care if I call the police."

"What police? Sam over on Ruby Island? Give me a break. He'd laugh himself silly. Even if you got him to listen to you, what would you tell him? That I made a couple of midnight trips to Hawthorne castle? I own the place, remember? I've got a perfect right to go there any time I want. You're the one who was illegally trespassing."

He was right, of course. She had absolutely nothing to report to any official. "Jared, something is going on, I know it."

"I don't care what you think you know so long as

you keep your mouth shut and don't give me any trouble. That means staying away from Hawthorne Castle. Understood?"

She jumped to her feet. "No, it is not understood. I want to know what's going on. I insist you tell me."

"Just because your curiosity is running wild doesn't mean I have to satisfy it, Kate."

"But if it's something illegal..."

"I've told you, it's not illegal."

"Why should I believe you?"

"I've never lied to you, have I?"

"Yes, you have. Last night is an instance that comes immediately to mind. You told me you had to go home early so David wouldn't be alone. But you didn't go home. You went to the castle."

"Oh, yeah. I forgot."

"You *forgot*? Forgot you lied to me? Very convenient."

Jared sipped his coffee. "I didn't actually lie to you, you know. I did have to get home early last night. But I allowed myself enough time to make the trip to the castle."

"I'm supposed to accept that as an explanation?" Kate yelped.

"You're really worked up about this, aren't you?"

"Yes, dammit, I am. I've got reason to be worked up. I've been lied to, misled and physically assaulted by the man with whom I'm having an affair."

"Let's not get carried away here. I didn't actually set out to assault you. It was dark in that hall and I wasn't sure who was coming up the steps. I just grabbed the first warm body that appeared. The next thing I knew, I was forced to defend myself against all two weeks' worth of your self-defense lessons. Which reminds me, you need a little work in some areas, Kate. I might be able to give you a couple of tips. I studied karate for a few years."

Kate folded her arms across her chest and stood stiffly in front of the entrance to the veranda. "I don't believe this. You're not going to explain any of it, are you?"

"No."

She whirled around and slammed her fist against the nearest wall. "You can't do this to me. I'm having an affair with you, dammit. That gives me some rights. I demand an explanation, Jared."

"Well, you're not going to get it, so you might as well calm down. The only thing you are going to get is my personal guarantee that what I'm doing is legal. You are also going to get a few strict instructions. From now on, you stay way from the castle."

"I could try cornering Max Butterfield and asking him what's going on." It was a weak threat, but it was all Kate had.

"Max left the island yesterday afternoon."

That stopped her for a second, but only a second. "I could tell Letty or the colonel what I've seen."

"Go ahead. They'll come straight to me and I'll tell them everything's under control. That will satisfy them. You'll just wind up making yourself look foolish."

"Because as long as you're in charge, everything's

just hunky-dory here on Amethyst Island, is that it? I don't believe this."

"Believe it." Jared set down his cup and leaned back in the leather chair. "It's the way things work around here."

"So I've been told." Kate massaged her temples and tried to clear her head. "This is crazy."

"Can't you trust me, Kate?" Jared asked gently.

"That's unfair," she snapped. "You know if the situation was reversed, you'd jump on me with both feet, demanding explanations."

"Only because I'd be worried about you getting yourself into trouble."

"Okay, so I'm worried about you."

He smiled grimly and put his feet up on the desk. "There's no need. I've been taking care of myself for a long time."

"Jared, I don't like this. You've been living out here beyond the reach of civilization for so long that you're starting to think you're a law unto yourself, the way Roger Hawthorne thought he was."

"Not quite. I haven't started locking people up in dungeons yet."

"That's not very funny. Roger did that?"

"Sure. He was the only law on the island and the bunch that worked for him was rough, to put it mildly. He occasionally needed a dungeon, so he had one built at the bottom of those stairs you were exploring this morning."

"That little cell? That's some sort of dungeon?" Kate's eyes widened. "I knew it. But there's more down there than just that barred room. I know there is. I saw the way the footprints just disappear near the wall."

"Did you?" He eyed her speculatively.

"There's something else down there, Jared."

"Yeah. There is. But it's got nothing to do with you. One of these days, I'll show you the whole place, honey, but not today. Not for a couple more weeks, at least. Until I give you the word, you are not going to set foot on the castle path."

"You can't stop me from going wherever I want to go."

"Yes, I can. Here on Amethyst, I can do just about anything I want."

She stared at him for a long, measuring moment and knew he was right. "You really mean that, don't you? You really think you can give me orders and make me obey them."

"Kate," he said wearily, "even if you went back to the castle, you wouldn't see anything more than you did this morning. There's nothing more to see except a few other empty rooms."

"Then why can't I go there and explore to my heart's content?"

"Because it's unsafe, that's why. I've told you that."

"It's more than just structurally unsafe, isn't it? Whatever you're involved in there is dangerous. I know it is."

Jared swung his feet down from the desk, his eyes narrowing. "Look, I've had enough of this. Whether you like it or not, I'm the boss around here. Hawthorne castle belongs to me. That makes it private property. I don't want you anywhere near it and that's final."

"And you really don't feel you owe me any explanations at all?" she asked in stunned, helpless disbelief.

"Just because I'm sleeping with you? No."

Kate looked at his implacable face and realized further argument was useless. Furious, she went to the door and yanked it open. "You arrogant, overbearing, dictatorial, son of a... You know something, Jared Hawthorne? You're no better than your ancestor. You're just a twentieth-century pirate who thinks he's lord of all he surveys."

She slammed the door on her way out. When she was safely back in her room, she cried for the first time since Harry had walked out the door.

On that occasion she had been feeling hurt and humiliated and very much a failure. This time it was much worse. This time she was afraid her heart might break.

SEVEN

Jared walked into the nearly empty bar that afternoon and realized immediately that the news of his quarrel with Kate had spread even faster than the news of his affair with her. He also knew that if it was all over the resort, it would be all over the island by now, too.

"Well, well, well, decided to come out of hiding, eh?" The colonel rested both hands on the bar and grinned in masculine commiseration. "Don't worry, it's safe enough in here for the moment. The lady's nowhere in sight. Haven't seen her all day."

"Is that right? And how do you know I've been in hiding?" Jared dropped onto a stool and hooked his foot over the brass rung.

"Lani was behind the front desk this morning when Kate came out of your office. I gather Ms Inskip looked more than mildly annoyed after her early morning interview. She didn't say anything, according to Lani, but it was obvious she'd just gone toe-to-toe with someone and the only other person in your office, Lani says, was you. You yourself have apparently been snapping off heads right and left all day. Everyone agrees that makes it official: you and Kate must have quarreled."

Jared swore, knowing there was no stopping the local rumor mill. "Is everyone else enjoying this as much as you are, Colonel?"

"Far as I can tell."

"Where's Kate?"

"I have no idea. Haven't seen her."

"She's probably sulking in her room. I'll give her a little while longer and then I'll go see if I can smooth a few feathers."

"You think it's going to be that easy?"

"She'll calm down. She's just a little pissed at the moment."

"I'd say she's more than a little pissed."

"Only because she lost the argument. She'll get over it."

"I wouldn't count on that happening anytime soon. I get the impression Ms Inskip is not accustomed to losing an argument. And since you're not exactly an expert at losing, either, I'd say we're in for a long siege."

"What's she going to do? Spend the rest of her vacation in her room? She's not that silly or irrational."

The colonel polished a glass and contemplated that. "She might decide there are more pleasant places to spend a vacation than Amethyst Island."

That jolted Jared. His jaw tightened. "You think she'd leave just because I put my foot down with her over something that was none of her business in the first place?"

"Is that what you did?"

"Yeah, that's what I did. Apparently she hasn't had too many people do that to her."

"I can see why," the colonel said. "As far as her getting ready to leave the island, I can't say for certain one way or the other. Haven't heard a thing on that score. Guess we'll find out soon enough, though, won't we? Hank will be making his usual afternoon run back to Ruby in about an hour. If she's on the plane we'll have our answer. A lot of people have a lot of money riding on it, you know."

"Who's handling the bets?" Jared asked, resigned to the inevitable.

"Jim at the front desk."

"Figures." The news irritated Jared but did not particularly surprise him. He was suddenly far more concerned about another matter. Until that moment it hadn't occurred to him that Kate might actually leave the island because of the quarrel. He thought about that possibility a moment longer and then stood up quickly. "See you later, Colonel."

"Where are you going?"

"To catch Hank. I want to make sure he knows he hasn't got a spare seat on that Cessna of his."

"Hank almost always has a spare seat on the afternoon hop."

"Not today he hasn't."

Twenty minutes later Jared drove swiftly back from the small paved strip that served as Amethyst

Island's airport. He killed the Jeep's engine in the resort driveway with a quick, savage motion of his hand.

He wasn't in a good mood, but he was momentarily satisfied. Hank Whitcomb had been willing to see reason the moment Jared had pointed out that there were other island pilots who wouldn't mind getting a guaranteed daily schedule between Amethyst and Ruby.

"Sure thing, Jared," Hank had said with a grin when Jared handed him enough cash to cover the cost of one empty seat to Ruby. "No seats available on this here flight. None whatsoever. Good luck with that little lady, pal. Sounds like she's got you running around in circles."

He was not running around in circles, Jared assured himself as he stalked into the lobby. He was simply drawing a few lines for a woman who needed them drawn.

He found the front desk vacant and promptly hit the bell to summon a clerk.

"What can I do for you?" asked the thin young man who emerged from the office. He had started talking before he realized who it was that stood at the front desk. When he saw Jared, he blinked a little nervously. "Oh, it's you, boss. Sorry, I was just checking something on the computer. We had some last-minute bookings."

Jared leaned his elbows on the polished desk and waved a twenty in front of the desk clerk's nose.

"Forget the last-minute bookings, Jim. I want to place a last-minute bet."

"Uh, sure thing, boss. Whatever you say." Jim smiled weakly. "What exactly did you want to bet on?"

"The same thing everyone else around here is betting on: whether or not Ms Inskip leaves with Hank this afternoon."

The clerk had the grace to turn red. He cleared his throat with a couple of coughs. "How did you want to place your bet, boss?"

"I've got twenty that says she won't be on the plane."

"Yes, sir. Twenty it is." The clerk leaned forward conspiratorially. "You know something the rest of us don't?"

"Of course not." Jared smiled grimly. "I just feel lucky."

"Hey, Dad, where have you been? I've been looking all over for you." David dashed down the hall and skidded to a halt as Jared walked into the house. The boy looked worried.

"I ran out to the strip for a few minutes. Had to talk to Hank." Jared ruffled his son's hair.

"You didn't take Kate out to the strip, did you?" David demanded, thoroughly alarmed now.

Jared scowled. "No, I did not take Kate out to the strip. Why?"

"'Cause everyone knows she's mad at you and

we're all afraid she's gonna leave on account of you yelled at her. It'll be all your fault if she goes, Dad."

"I did not yell at her. And where did you hear about her being mad at me?"

"Everyone says so. Hey, it's not because of that bet you and I made about her cooking, is it? Is she mad because we did that?"

"No, it's not because of the bet. Kate doesn't even know there was a bet. And if the subject comes up I want it clear that it was all your idea."

"You're the one who said she probably couldn't cook," David reminded him. "You bet me a dollar she couldn't, remember?"

"Yeah, but you're the one who suggested we con her into fixing dinner so we could find out for sure. You are also the guy who won a buck off me because she could make pizza. I'd appreciate it if you would not forget your part in all this."

David chewed his lower lip. "She'd probably really get mad if she ever found out, huh?"

"Yes," Jared said, "I think she would be very mad."

David sighed. "She sure made a great pizza, didn't she? You said she'd probably burn it, but she didn't."

"Pizza is probably the only thing she knows how to cook. I don't think Ms Inskip is the homey type."

"Anyone who can make good pizza can probably make lots of good stuff."

"Maybe," Jared agreed cautiously.

"Think she'll leave the island because you yelled at her?"

Jared lost what was left of his patience. "I told you, I did not yell at her, and no, Kate's not going to be leaving the island. Not today, at any rate."

David's expression relaxed instantly. "That's great. In that case, I'm going to win another buck."

"I should have guessed." Jared swore under his breath but without much heat. "You'd think everyone around here could find something more interesting to bet on than the status of my love life."

David's gaze widened with interest. "Is that what you have, Dad? A love life?"

"Had. Past tense."

Jared went into the kitchen and dug a cold beer out of the refrigerator. Then he walked out onto the veranda, dropped onto a lounger and started wondering how he was going to get his love life back. It was amazing how fast a man could get used to having a certain prickly little broad around.

Kate packed and unpacked her suitcase three times before sinking dejectedly onto the bed. She knew she ought to leave on the afternoon flight. If she had an ounce of self-respect, not to mention common sense, she would get off the island. She could not possibly stay here after what had happened this morning.

It amazed her to think she had spent years fantasizing about pirates. Having met one in the flesh, she now realized they were an infuriating breed. Give her a nice, sensitive, understanding, *civilized* male any day.

The knock on the door brought her head up with a

start and her heart leaped. As she went to answer the summons, she steeled herself to be firm. If this was Jared come to apologize and explain his actions, she would not make it easy for him. The man deserved to do some groveling. Head high, she opened the door.

"Oh, hi, Letty."

"I take it you were expecting someone else?" Letty's expression was one of sympathetic female-to-female understanding.

"Not exactly expecting, more like entertaining a fleeting hope. Come on in."

Letty walked in and glanced at the open suitcases. "So you're going to leave," she said softly. "I wondered if you might be thinking of it."

"To be honest, I haven't made up my mind."

"Better hurry." Letty glanced at her watch. "Hank takes off in half an hour."

"The thing is, I hate to let that arrogant, dictatorial clod run me off the island this easily." Kate started to rehang some of her clothing. "It goes against the grain."

"Said arrogant, dictatorial clod being Jared?"

"Yes."

"Good." Letty settled into one of the chairs near the screened window. "Glad to hear it. The staff is taking bets, and I've got five dollars riding on your decision."

Kate wrinkled her nose. "There's certainly not much privacy on this island, is there?"

"Afraid not."

"Everyone knows I'm furious with Jared?"

"Uh-huh. Believe me, no matter which way they're betting, they're all praying you'll stay."

"Why?"

"Because no one wants to deal with Jared's temper after you leave. He's in one heck of a bad mood and they all figure it's going to get worse if you run off."

"I'm supposed to do everyone a favor and soothe the savage beast?" Kate was outraged anew. "Forget it. The quarrel was one hundred percent his fault."

"Was it?"

"It most certainly was." Kate rehung another dress. "Furthermore, I have absolutely no intention of apologizing to the man. But you can go collect your winnings, if you like, because I've just decided for certain that I'm not going to let him chase me off this island. I came here for a vacation, by heaven. I'm going to get one. Lord knows I've paid enough for it."

Letty grinned. "Somehow I rather thought you'd take that attitude."

"Don't look so delighted, Letty. I'm not hanging around so that I can placate Jared. I've got better things to do on my vacation. The big affair is at an end."

"Did you inform Jared yet?"

"He'll find out soon enough."

"Can't wait." Letty got up and headed for the door.

"Where are you going?"

"Now that I've got a little inside information, I thought I'd go double my bet."

Kate stared as the door closed behind her friend.

All in all, she did not think she was getting cured of her stress problems.

That night Kate dressed for the evening ahead as if she were preparing to go into battle. She went through everything she had brought with her and finally selected a flame-colored gown with an artfully draped bodice and a full, flouncy, flirty skirt. A pair of red heels and a silver collar at her throat completed the effect. She surveyed herself in the mirror and decided she had the look she wanted—cool, regal and totally self-contained.

When she walked into the crowded bar for an aperitif, she could feel the speculation, approval and open relief emanating from the staff. The colonel arched one thick brow and inclined his head in a silent salute. Kate smiled demurely and took one of the fan-backed chairs near the railing. A few minutes later a rum-and-fruit concoction materialized at her elbow. She looked up to smile at the waitress.

"Glad you didn't leave," the woman said in a low voice.

"Don't tell me, let me guess. You had a bet riding on my plans for the future, too?" Kate was long past the outraged stage. She had moved on to a sort of fatalistic acceptance of the inevitable.

"I bet ten dollars you wouldn't be going back to Ruby with Hank Whitcomb," the waitress admitted, "but that's not the real reason I'm glad you stayed."

"You think I'm going to somehow wave my magic wand and put Jared back into a good mood?"

The waitress laughed. "You'd have the eternal gratitude of the entire staff of Crystal Cove."

"Has it occurred to anyone that the only reason I might have hung around here is so that Jared can exert himself to put *me* back into a pleasant frame of mind?"

The waitress considered that angle. She appeared to have trouble grasping the concept. "Is that why you stayed? To bring Jared to his knees?"

"You look doubtful."

The waitress's smile broadened. "Let's just say it should be interesting. Good luck, Ms Inskip. Oh, and I just finished your last book. It was great. Loved that part where the hero goes into the bedroom thinking the heroine is going to be meekly waiting for him in bed and she dumps the chamber pot over his head instead."

"I'm glad you enjoyed it."

Kate allowed the waitress's parting remark to warm her as she sat gazing out at the darkening sea. But the good feeling didn't last long. It was obvious everyone at Crystal Cove was finding the situation between herself and Jared vastly entertaining, but Kate knew better. There was nothing funny about her quarrel with Jared; this was no amusing battle of the sexes. The stakes were too high.

She went cold whenever she allowed herself to speculate on what Jared might be involved in up at Hawthorne Castle.

Jared had the natural authority and innate arrogance of a man who was accustomed to running his own domain, but she knew him well enough by now to know he was neither vicious nor totally unreasonable. Vicious, unreasonable men did not build thriving resorts capable of supporting the economy of an entire island. Vicious, unreasonable men did not incur the kind of loyalty and friendship Jared had locally.

Or did they?

Something serious was going on up at Hawthorne Castle, and Jared was deeply involved. He did not want her anywhere near the place and as far as Kate could tell, there could be only one reason for forbidding her to take the castle path: Kate was very much afraid Jared was following in the footsteps of Roger Hawthorne, and because she was also very much afraid she was in love with him, she knew she had to stop him.

She was lost in thought when a shadow fell across the table. She looked up, half expecting to see Jared standing there, but it was Jeff Taylor who was smiling hopefully down at her.

"I see you're alone tonight. Mind if I join you?" He was dressed in a pair of slacks and a flower-printed aloha shirt. His red hair was still damp from a shower.

Kate smiled. "Not at all."

Jeff's smile widened with satisfaction. "Thanks." He took the chair across from her and lifted a hand to catch the waitress's attention. "Haven't been able to catch you alone since the night of the masquerade ball. You been hanging out with the local boss man, I hear. How come he's left you on your own tonight?"

"I'm on vacation," Kate said. "I hang out with whoever I want to hang out with."

"Hope that means me tonight."

Out of the corner of her eye, Kate saw Jared saunter through the door and head for the bar. She tensed, preparing for a scene. "Why not?" she said, smiling brilliantly.

Several hours later Kate finally decided Jared was not going to make a scene, after all. She told herself she was glad, but some small, very primitive part of her was hurt, she had to admit.

It was not that she didn't enjoy herself with Jeff Taylor. They had dinner together and danced afterward. Jeff was charming, funny and more than willing to follow her lead. When she eventually pleaded weariness and said she wanted to go to her room, he quickly volunteered to walk her back through the gardens. She wondered briefly if she would have trouble with him at the door, but when she dismissed him gently, he went with good grace.

"Maybe we can do this again," he murmured, brushing a quick, light kiss across her cheek.

"Maybe." She smiled a good-night sort of smile that made no promises. Behind her the room was shrouded in darkness.

"Say, you want to go snorkeling in the cove tomorrow morning?"

She hesitated and then asked herself why not. She

was supposed to be on vacation, after all. "Sounds great."

Jeff grinned. "I'll meet you right after breakfast."

"That will be fine."

Kate smiled again and then closed the door gently but firmly in his face. She turned around and walked into the room without bothering to switch on the light. She went to the screened wall and stood looking out at the silvered sea. She was learning to love the island night. The fragrant, velvet air drifted through the open windows, caressing her and bringing back poignant memories of the nights she had spent in Jared's arms.

The familiar feeling of awareness went through her and she hugged herself. It was ridiculous, but she could almost feel him nearby. There was that curious tingling at the back of her neck...Kate gasped and whirled around.

"Lucky for all of us you didn't invite Taylor into the room," Jared said from the shadows of the bed. "Could have been a little awkward trying to explain the crowd in here."

"*Jared.*" Kate took hold of herself immediately. "What are you doing here?"

"What do you think I'm doing here?" His hand moved negligently, and the pale moonlight glinted off the brandy snifter he was holding. He was propped up against a couple of pillows, wearing a pair of low-slung jeans and nothing else.

"How did you get in here?"

"I own the place, remember? I have a key."

Kate drew a deep breath, unable to move. This was not fear, she told herself firmly. She was just feeling naturally wary of the big, dangerous man on her bed. "Did you stop by to apologize and explain yourself?"

Jared sipped meditatively from the snifter. "No. What about you? Finished playing games with Taylor?"

"I'll play games with whoever I feel like playing games with."

"Then we have a problem, don't we?"

"I don't see why. You and I are no longer involved, remember? We had a major quarrel this morning. That was the end of our famous affair as far as I'm concerned."

"You're lying. If you thought things were over between us, you would have bought a ticket on the afternoon plane to Ruby. You didn't even try."

"I said things were over between us, I didn't say my vacation was over."

"Go ahead and tell yourself whatever you like. We both know you're still here because of what's happening between us."

"You are so damned arrogant."

"And you're not?"

"Not like you," Kate shot back.

He laughed softly and sat up on the side of the bed. He put the snifter down on the end table and got to his feet, facing her. "You're more like me than you want to admit and that's why we've got a few problems. But I'm beginning to think we can fix all that."

She instinctively stepped back as he came around

the end of the bed and started toward her. Then she
refused to retreat any farther. Her chin lifted even as
she felt herself turning hot and vibrant with the fierce
emotions coursing through her.

"Now just one blasted minute, Jared Hawthorne."

"Let's get something clear right from the start. This
is just between you and me," Jared said. "You want
to go to war, we'll go to war. You want to make love,
we'll make love. But we don't involve any third parties. No more Jeff Taylors."

"You really are a pirate, aren't you?"

"If I'm a pirate, you were born to be a pirate's
woman." His hands closed over her shoulders and
his mouth found hers in a searing kiss.

He was right, Kate acknowledged silently as she
felt the passion rising swiftly; some part of her had
been born to respond to him. He was the man she had
been waiting for all her life. Her arms went around
his neck and she shoved her fingers through his thick,
dark hair.

Jared exhaled heavily, his body going hard at her
touch. "I knew when you didn't try to get on that
plane today that you realized this was special." He
pulled her down onto the bed and sprawled across
her. "Neither one of us can walk away from it now."

His arrogance appalled her. "All right," Kate said,
looking up at him through her lashes, "I'll admit the
sex is good. And I've heard it's a great cure for stress.
I might as well enjoy it."

Jared's eyes glittered with sudden anger and his

hands tightened on her. "It isn't just the sex and you know it."

"What else is there? It's not as if there's a lot of trust or love between us."

"Damn you, stop trying to manipulate me. I'm not the kind of man you can push and prod until I collapse in a heap of jelly and tell you whatever you want to hear. One of these days you're going to learn that."

"Just as you're going to have to learn that I'm not the kind of sweet, soft, meek little woman who will let you pat her on the head and tell her to mind her own business."

He stared down at her, his mouth inches from her own, his hands locked on her shoulders. "One of us is going to have to back down and I can tell you right now, it won't be me, Kate. I know what I'm doing and I know what's best for you. You're going to have to trust me and that's final."

"Nothing is final," she told him, pulling his head down to hers. "But there's no point talking about it tonight."

"On that we agree."

His mouth took hers once more in a kiss that demanded everything from her. It was as if he had decided that in place of the capitulation he could not quite wring from her, he would take her very soul instead.

Kate trembled with the force of her passion, clinging to Jared as he thrust her legs apart with his own. Her red skirt foamed high up on her thighs. He freed her mouth with a husky groan and buried his lips in the curve of her shoulder.

She felt his hands on the zipper of the red dress and a moment later the silky material was being pushed down over her hips. She was alive with her own desire and infinitely aware of his. The combination was electric. Kate wondered why there were no visible sparks flaring in the darkened room. The invisible ones were everywhere, igniting a wildfire.

Jared's hands moved hungrily on her, tugging off the red dress, the red shoes and the panty hose. When she was wearing nothing except the silver collar and moonlight he sat up and unfastened his jeans. He stepped out of them in a series of quick, jerky movements that spoke volumes about his restless impatience. When he was free of the denims he stood beside the bed for a long moment, staring down at her. His body was heavy with arousal.

"You want me, don't you?" he asked.

"Yes."

"Don't ever again say it's just good sex," he ordered as he came down beside her. His palm closed over her breast.

"That really bothered you, didn't it? Why?"

"Because it's a lie and I won't let you lie to me."

"But it's all right for you to lie to me?" she asked.

"I've never lied to you, but there are some things you don't need to know." He stroked his hands through her hair. "You'll just have to learn to trust me."

"Jared—"

"Hush. Not now." He cut off her words with a hot kiss, his tongue plunging between her lips. His fingers roamed over her, awakening her nipples and moving lower to find the dampening warmth between her legs.

Kate's head was spinning with the euphoric excitement. She touched him wonderingly, loving the feel of his beautifully contoured back and the sleek muscles of his thighs. She let her nails slip into the rough hair below his waist and when she found the hard, thrusting shape of him she circled him gently.

"Yes," Jared said, his voice hoarse with barely controlled need. "Touch me. Harder. That's it. So good. So damned good."

She raised herself on one elbow and pushed him gently onto his back. He went over easily, watching her through hooded eyes as she leaned down to kiss his throat.

His fingers kneaded her shoulders as she trailed small, damp kisses over his bare skin. She felt his hips lifting urgently against her.

In this, at least, there was totally honesty between them, Kate told herself. Jared made no effort to conceal his desire. The wanting in his eyes was blatant and implacable.

The excitement roared through both of them. Kate could feel her own passion feeding off Jared's. The energy of their lovemaking dampened their skins with as much perspiration as if they had been engaged in a battle.

Jared, apparently growing impatient with the

sweet warfare, finally shifted onto his back and pulled Kate across his thighs. He guided her down, pushing himself slowly up into her softness until he was deep inside.

Kate sank her nails into his skin, closed her eyes and gave herself up to the white-hot passion. Jared's hands were all over her, moving on the insides of her thighs and up into the hidden places. He seemed to know exactly how to touch her. His fingers thrummed gently and she cried out.

"Come on, honey. Let me see you come apart for me. You know you will. You know you want it. That's it. *That's it*. Tight. Tighter. So beautiful. *Yes*."

Kate gasped and collapsed against his chest as the sweet, shattering finale took her. Jared's damp hands clenched into her rounded buttocks and he lifted himself against her one more time. He bared his teeth, caught his breath and shuddered heavily.

Afterward they lay together for a long while without speaking. Kate had her head on Jared's shoulder and his arm was around her, pinning her close to the length of him.

"I can't stay," Jared said at last, his reluctance to leave clear in his voice. "I have to get back to the house. Beth won't be able to watch David all night."

"I know."

"He won a dollar today betting you wouldn't leave the island."

"I think everyone had a bet on whether or not I'd get on that plane."

"They all wanted you to stay."

Kate sighed and moved her head restlessly against the pillow. "They don't understand. They think we had a simple lovers' quarrel and that's all there was to it."

"It *was* just a simple quarrel. Given your stubbornness, I expect there will be plenty of others."

"Not a cheerful thought."

"We don't have to argue, you know." Jared sat up slowly and reached for his jeans. "I'd much rather make love with you."

She lay watching him as he dressed. "Would you?"

He fastened his jeans and leaned over the bed to cage her between his hands. "Yes," he said. "I would. But if you want to fight occasionally, I'll fight with you. I'm an accommodating man, Kate."

"Gee, thanks."

"There's just one thing you ought to know before you launch too many more battles."

"What's that?"

"You can't end any of them by getting on a plane and flying home."

"Who's going to stop me?" As usual, she could not resist rising to the bait.

Jared smiled slowly in the shadows. "Take a wild guess." He kissed her again, straightened and walked out the door.

EIGHT

Kate surfaced, pushed back her mask and snorkel and laughed up at Jeff Taylor, who stood in the water beside her. "This is great," she said. "I could get used to doing this every morning before going to work."

"If you think this is good, you should try the diving." He indicated his gear on the beach. "Fantastic. I'm going out in a while. Going to do a little underwater photography."

Kate nodded as she started toward shore. "It sounds fascinating." She wondered if she could write off the expense of diving lessons if she used the information in a book.

That thought unfortunately only served to remind her that soon she would be returning to Seattle. She tried to push the unwelcome realization aside as she walked up onto the beach. She halted beside Jeff's diving gear, eyeing the yellow-and-black wet suit.

"Do you need a suit for diving in these warm waters?"

Jeff nodded, picking up a towel. "You do when

you're going to be in the water for a long time. Any water, no matter how warm, saps your body heat after a while."

"Who will you be diving with today?"

"No one. I go by myself."

"Aren't you supposed to always dive with a buddy?" Kate dried her hair with the towel.

"Technically. But I know what I'm doing in the water and I prefer to go down by myself. I don't take stupid chances. Do me a favor, though, and don't tell the resort management I dive alone, okay? Someone is almost bound to feel obligated to give me a lecture on the subject of diving safety, and I hate lectures."

Kate smiled. "I won't mention it. Be careful, though."

"I'm always careful."

"Have a good dive and thanks for joining me this morning." She draped her towel around her neck, turned and waved as she started up the beach.

"Maybe I'll catch up with you later in the bar," Jeff called.

"Maybe."

A few minutes later Kate halted at the top of the path and looked back. Jeff was busy adjusting his wet suit. She waited awhile longer and watched as he strapped on the rest of his gear and finally slipped into the water. He disappeared at once. The whole business looked like a lot of fun, Kate decided. If she lived here on Amethyst, she would definitely learn how to dive.

But she did not live here on the island, and somehow she couldn't work up a lot of interest in diving back home in the cold, dark waters of Puget Sound. She had gotten accustomed to warm, clear, turquoise seas.

You can't have everything, Kate reminded herself. The affair with Jared would eventually end and she would be left with real-life memories to match her dreams. There were a lot of women who never even got that much.

She was contemplating the dismal prospect of returning home alone when she rounded a corner into the hotel gardens and nearly collided with Max Butterfield.

"I beg your pardon," Kate apologized quickly and hurriedly stepped back. She looked with chagrin at the damp spots she had left on Max's pristine white shirt.

"Please don't concern yourself." Max fastidiously brushed his shirt and then the white pants. He was obviously not pleased with the wet patches she had left behind, but he managed a gracious smile. "Should have been watching where I was going. Been swimming, I see?"

"Yes. Great morning for it. But then, I guess all the mornings around here are pretty terrific, aren't they?"

"Endless paradise," Max said, glancing over her shoulder and out to sea. "Hard to believe one could ever actually tire of it, isn't it? Would you care to join me for a cup of coffee on the pool terrace, Ms Inskip?

We can talk shop. It's been a long time since I conversed with a fellow writer. One tends to lose touch."

Kate hesitated and then nodded, unable to think of a suitable excuse. "All right. That sounds nice. Thank you."

They made their way through the open lobby to the tiled terrace that surrounded the pool. A waiter in sunglasses took their order and returned with a silver pot of coffee, two croissants and a Bloody Mary for Max.

"When did you first come out here to the islands, Max?" Kate buttered a croissant and popped a flaky bite into her mouth.

"So long ago that I can no longer remember the exact date, but I do remember the marvelous sense of adventure I felt at the time. Quite extraordinary. Everything seemed so exotic, you know. I was certain I was destined to be famous and in the little biographical notes at the end of my books it would be mentioned quite casually that I lived and worked on a tropical island."

"That sort of thing always makes a nice touch in an author's biography," Kate conceded. "Gives the writer a larger-than-life image, doesn't it?

"It does, indeed, and when I first arrived here I fully intended to live a larger-than-life sort of life. But somehow time has gone by so much more quickly than I had planned. My novel is still waiting to be written, but in the meantime I have had to support myself with small jobs on the side and here and there a travel piece." Max shrugged massively and polished off the rest of his croissant. "Life seldom turns out as one had thought it would, does it? But one learns to adapt. Tell me about yourself, Ms Inskip."

"Not much to tell. I live and work in Seattle. I've managed to make a living doing something I love, so I consider myself lucky." *You can't have everything.*

"You are. I consider people like you and Jared Hawthorne extremely fortunate, and I must confess I envy you. I cannot tell you how much I envy you. You are both making a living doing what you love."

And we both worked hard to earn our luck, Kate thought, glancing around at the beautiful resort and thinking of what it must have cost Jared in terms of time, work and money. Then she reflected on the frustrations she had endured in her writing career and recalled the number of rejections she had received over the years.

It was odd to think that she and Jared actually had something in common in terms of their success. Neither of them had been handed anything on a silver platter. They had both paid their dues.

"I still have a few faint hopes," Max went on, sipping his Bloody Mary. "One never gives up entirely, I suppose. Once in a while we are fortunate enough to be given a golden opportunity to reshape our private destinies. I'm keeping an eye out for such a chance."

"I wish you the best of luck, Max." Kate smiled at him, willing herself to be a little more understanding. She knew how she would have felt by now if she had never gotten published.

"Thank you, my dear. You are very kind."

* * *

"I saw you on the terrace having coffee with Kate this morning," Jared said as he sat down across from Max in the bar. "Why?"

"So blunt. Are you jealous of me, by any chance? I am truly flattered. When one reaches my age, jealousy from a younger man is always welcomed, even if there is no cause."

"You know damned well this isn't a question of jealousy." Jared leaned back in the fan chair and studied Max through narrowed eyes. "What did you talk about?"

"Nothing that need concern you, my boy. We merely chatted about our shared interests."

"What shared interests?"

"Writing."

"Don't give me that. You haven't written a thing except one or two obscure travel articles in all the years I've known you, Max."

Max's eyes went cold. "That does not mean I have no intention of writing again. I was a good writer once, Jared. Editors said I had potential. A great deal of it."

"Well, you're in another business now, aren't you?" Jared was feeling annoyed and when he got annoyed, he got a little ruthless. "And you've dragged me into it, too. The sooner this whole thing is over, the better. I don't like it."

"You've made your feelings on the subject quite clear right from the start." Max smiled benignly. "My supervisors are aware of your attitude. They understand that you are doing us a very big favor and they have asked me to convey their appreciation."

"Screw their appreciation. I want this thing brought to a quick end and then I don't want to hear from you or your supervisors again. When you write up your final report, Max, I want you to make it clear that there will be no more favors from me. We're even."

Max lifted his glass of rum in a short, mocking toast. "Understood. No more favors."

"When is it going to be over, Max? I'm tired of being kept on the line. This is my island and I don't like you and your friends playing games on it. I want a day and a time."

"Calm yourself, my friend. Everything is scheduled for the regular cruise ship day at the end of the month. Our little fish will swallow the hook at that time, as planned."

Jared stood up. "The sooner the better."

"I could not agree with you more," Max said. His gaze was on the sea as he sipped his drink.

Jared started to walk away, paused and turned back. He leaned down, one hand planted on the table and spoke softly. "No more cozy little chats with Kate, Max. I don't want her to be touched by any of this, not even indirectly."

Max was both amused and offended. "You think I am so unprofessional as to let something slip to a pretty lady?"

"I think," Jared said, spacing his words for emphasis, "that the pretty lady is also pretty smart and it wouldn't take much to make her curious. Stay away from her."

This time Jared did not pause as he walked away from the table. He nodded briefly at the colonel on the way out of the bar and then headed for the lobby.

He spotted Kate and David as soon as he crossed the small lagoon bridge. They were standing together looking up at one of the watercolors on the wall. They didn't notice him right away and he stopped to watch them for a moment.

David was talking very seriously about the painting, and Kate had her head tilted in the familiar way that meant she was paying close attention. Jared studied the graceful line of her throat and shoulder and something deep within him tightened as memories of the previous night trickled back. She had only to be in the same room with him to arouse him, he realized. The intensity of his feelings amazed him. She stirred a part of his nature that he had never fully explored and the knowledge that he could feel such an aching need at this stage of his life was unsettling.

She was so different from Gabriella in every way. His wife had been like the watercolor on the wall, a soft, gentle creation of pastels and light. Kate was vibrant and strong, full of color that was so hot and bright that it could, on occasion, singe a man's fingers.

But what was life without a few burned fingers, Jared asked himself with an inner smile as he went toward Kate and his son.

"What are you two up to this morning?" he asked as he came to a halt beside them.

"Hi, Dad. I was just telling Kate that it was my mother who painted this picture."

Kate smiled gently at Jared, her eyes searching his face. "Your wife was a very talented woman."

Jared glanced at the soft seascape and nodded briefly. "Yes, she was. She did all the lobby paintings."

"That's what Dave was just telling me."

"Yeah, I was explaining it to her, Dad. But I got to go now. Carl's expecting me. See you guys later." David dashed out of the lobby and across the small bridge.

Jared watched his son until the boy was out of sight and then he turned back to find Kate studying him. "I told you once, Dave doesn't really remember his mother, but he takes a lot of pride in knowing she did these paintings. It gives him a way of feeling his connection to her."

Kate nodded. "I understand. She must have been a very lovely woman to have created such lovely art."

"She was." Jared glanced at his watch. "What do you say we go get some lunch in the restaurant? It's almost noon."

"All right."

A few minutes later Kate put down her menu and looked across the table at Jared. "I'm very different from her, aren't I?"

Jared, who had just been wondering why Kate had been so abnormally silent for so long, suddenly understood. "Night and day," he said casually. He plucked the menu out of Kate's fingers and turned to the waitress who had bustled up to take their orders. "Bring us the fresh tuna, Nancy. I know Marty got a delivery this morning."

"You bet, boss. Be right back."

"I didn't come all this way to have tuna fish," Kate complained.

Jared grinned. "The difference between fresh tuna and canned tuna fish is also night and day. Relax, you're going to love it, especially the way Marty does it."

"Is that why you're sleeping with me, Jared? Because I don't remind you of Gabriella?"

Jared drummed his fingers on the table and wondered why it was women asked such ridiculous questions. "Are you sleeping with me because I don't resemble your ex-husband?"

She turned faintly pink, which surprised him.

"Never mind," Kate said, moving a few inches back from the table in a small action that said more than words she was pulling back from the entire conversation. "I shouldn't have asked you such a personal question." She smiled brightly. "I understand there's a cruise boat coming in next week."

"We get a ship through every few weeks. And the answer is no, I'm not sleeping with you because you are so different from Gabriella. I'm sleeping with you because you're you and you have a way of making me get as hard as an eighteen-year-old kid every time you're in the vicinity."

"Last night you said there was more to our relationship than just sex."

Jared realized he had not phrased his reassurance in the best possible way. "Kate, don't twist my words. I meant what I said last night and I mean what I'm saying now. I like going to bed with you and I like being with you when we're not in bed, even when you snap at me. Look, I'm not good at this kind of conversation. Could we change the subject?"

She propped her elbows on the table, laced her fingers and rested her chin on the back of her hands. Her eyes were very clear and green as she looked at him. "Of course, Mr. Hawthorne. Whatever you say, Mr. Hawthorne. Far be it from me to try to dictate our conversation. What would you like to discuss, Mr. Hawthorne?"

Jared swore softly. "You're mad at me again, aren't you? I was right the first time I met you. You are one prickly broad."

"Yes," Kate said. "I am a bit prickly. But that doesn't seem to keep you from wanting to climb into bed with me. An insightful observer could conclude that my prickliness might be one of the things that attracts you to me and you just don't want to admit it to yourself because you decided long ago you liked sweet, biddable, mild-mannered women."

"I don't think I followed the logic there, but don't bother running it by me again. I'm sure I'd get just as lost a second time. What are you going to do this afternoon?"

"Read some more of Amelia Cavendish's diary."

"Working your way through it, hmm?"

"It's fascinating."

"Only to a woman. I told you I couldn't get through it, even if she was the wife of a distant ancestor of mine. All that nonsense about her social life in England in the beginning and later that endless litany of complaints about the way Roger Hawthorne treated her. I never bothered to finish."

"Then you missed a lot of the good parts. She had legitimate grounds for all those complaints about your ancestor. He treated her abominably. First he woos her and then abandons her without so much as a goodbye note and then he returns three years later and expects her to marry him. When she doesn't instantly leap into his arms, he kidnaps her, brings her out here and forces her to marry him. Yes, I'd say she had a reason to gripe."

Jared laughed. "I'll let you in on a little secret. Roger's journal contains a couple of references to what he called his sharp-tongued little shrew. I gather she made life hell for him on board ship after he kidnapped her. He said at one point in the journal that he was probably the only man alive who could claim to have been nagged halfway around the world. Amelia complained about everything from the food on board ship to the way Hawthorne made a living."

"Amelia did not approve of his chosen profession," Kate said austerely.

"I gather she made that real clear. You know, you're beginning to remind me of her in more ways than one. I'm starting to appreciate just what poor Roger had to go through." Jared broke off as the tuna arrived. When the waitress disappeared again he looked up from his plate to find Kate studying him with her intelligent eyes. "What's the matter?"

"Nothing."

"Then eat your fish."

"Yes, sir."

"Do us both a favor and don't start baiting me today, okay?"

She shrugged. "Okay. Why did Roger Hawthorne leave England so suddenly the first time?"

"A little trouble resulting from a duel. He killed his opponent and had to get out of the country in a hurry. Dueling was illegal. There would have been a hell of a scandal for his family if he'd been caught."

"Why didn't he take the time to explain that to Amelia?"

"He left her a note explaining everything and asking her to wait for him, according to the journal. But apparently she never got the message or if she did, she didn't pay any attention."

"Really?" Kate's eyes were riveted on his face. "He left her a note? She knew nothing about any note."

"And didn't believe him three years later when he tried to explain. So he gave up explaining and kidnapped her instead."

"Very interesting," Kate mused. "There's no mention of a missed message in Amelia's journal."

"Like I said, she didn't believe Roger's story."

Jared looked up, seeing a golden opportunity to make a point. "She didn't *trust* him."

"How could she? The man was a pirate."

"Depends on your point of view. He didn't attack English ships. Just those of England's enemies. Enjoy your swim this morning?"

"Yes."

"You went snorkeling with Taylor, didn't you?"

"Yes." She forked up her tuna and sampled it tentatively, then nodded in approval.

Jared sighed and put down his fork. "Did you do it just to show me that you could get away with seeing Taylor after I told you I didn't want you hanging around with him?"

"No. I went swimming with him because I had already made the arrangement last night. You probably heard me make it, since you were lying on my bed eavesdropping at the time."

"You're not really interested in him, are you?" Jared was sure of that, which was the main reason he hadn't gone down to the cove this morning and interrupted the snorkeling activity.

"No, I'm not seriously interested in him. He's a nice guy who asked me to swim with him, and I'm supposed to be enjoying myself on vacation, so I went."

"Meaning you don't enjoy yourself with me?"

"I wouldn't say that. I like being with you when you're not grilling me or giving me orders or telling me to mind my own business. Unfortunately, that leaves a very small amount of time in which I can actually enjoy myself."

"Now I know how Roger Hawthorne felt when he realized he'd kidnapped a professional shrew."

"But the good time we do have together makes it all worth it," Kate concluded, her eyes flashing with feminine mischief.

Jared felt himself slipping under the spell of her provocative smile. He took a firm grip on himself and picked up his fork. This was neither the time nor the place to take her into his arms. He had work to do this afternoon. "All right, I'm ready to change the subject again."

"What would you like to discuss now? Ready to tell me what's going on up at the castle?"

"No, dammit." His temper erupted in a flash. The woman did not know when to quit. "And furthermore, I don't want to hear one more word about it. Clear?"

"Clear." She went back to eating and made no effort to introduce another subject.

Jared gave her five minutes of silence. Then he could no longer resist asking the question that had been at the back of his mind for several days. "I'm not like him at all, am I?"

She did not pretend to misunderstand. "My ex-husband? No, you're not like him at all. As you said, night and day."

He heard himself ask the next question before he had the good sense to think about what he was saying. "If you were ever to get married again, would you want someone like him? I mean someone like the man you thought he was when you married him? A sensitive, literary type? A guy with the soul of a poet or whatever it was you thought he had going for him?"

"Nope." Kate worked steadily on her tuna, apparently relishing every bite.

"I see." Jared found himself stewing in unaccustomed frustration. He hadn't wanted to ask the question in the first place, but having asked it, he had certainly expected a more complete answer than the one he had gotten. Kate was normally chatty as hell. "Do you, uh, know what you'd want the second time around?"

"No, but I expect I'll know it when I see it. Think you'll ever find someone who will fill Gabriella's shoes?"

That startled him. "I don't know." He frowned down at his tuna, trying to sort through his jumbled thoughts. "I'm not sure if that's really what I want, anyway. I used to think it was. But maybe it's not such a good idea. Lately, I've started wondering. I loved her. If she were still alive, I would still love her. But she's gone and I've done some changing and nothing stays the same, does it?"

"No." Kate smiled with a curious understanding. "That's the one sure thing in life. Nothing stays the same."

Jared nodded and then found himself saying aloud something he had never admitted to a living soul. "I had to be so careful with Gabby. She was very fragile.

So gentle. You could crush her with just a look. I treated her like rare crystal most of the time, but once in a while I didn't and then I'd feel guilty for days."

"I know what that kind of guilt is like. I wasn't always gentle enough with my husband," Kate said. "I would get impatient with him. His ego was so fragile and he used to get so depressed so easily. I don't think I was as understanding and compassionate as I should have been. It must have been hard on him watching me get successfully published while he kept accumulating rejections. Especially when he was convinced that what he was writing was infinitely more important than what I wrote."

Jared let the silence that followed her comment hang for a while. He realized he felt at peace with Kate for the first time that day. He replayed his own words in his head and saw the truth in them. Somewhere along the line he had stopped looking for a replacement for Gabriella. He wanted a wife, but he wanted someone who was a unique individual, a person in her own right, not a clone of Gabby.

"You really don't know what you want in a second husband?" Jared asked again.

"Like I said, I'm sure I'll know it when I see it."

That comment shattered his feeling of being at peace with her. He scowled across the table, annoyed. "What are you expecting to happen? You think some guy will walk into your life and you'll take one look and know he's the right man?"

"Sure. Why not?"

"You know what your problem is? You've written one too many romance novels," Jared muttered.

"Well?" Letty demanded a few days later when she happened across Kate curled in a shaded lounger. "Fill me in on the latest. How's Amelia doing with her pirate?"

Kate glanced up from the diary in her lap. "Whipping him into shape, I'm happy to say. She locked him out of her bedroom on her wedding night because he showed up drunk after too much carousing with his crew. She made it stick, too. Mostly because Roger was too drunk to find the key, which she had wisely hidden."

"I love it. What happened next?" Letty sat down nearby and poured herself a glass of iced tea from a pitcher Kate had ordered earlier.

"Roger was too embarrassed the next day to admit he hadn't made it into his wife's bedroom. So he tried acting as if everything was normal between himself and Amelia. Pretended there wasn't a thing in the world wrong. Unfortunately Amelia fell for the act. She went for a walk with him down to a secluded little cove." Kate wondered privately if it was the same cove where Jared had first made love to her.

"I'll bet Amelia soon found herself flat on her back in the sand."

"Eventually. It wasn't as bad as it sounds, though. Here's how she puts it:

Roger apologized very prettily for his uncouth behavior of the previous night and began a very learned discussion concerning the marital obligations of husbands and wives. I informed him that I was very well aware of those obligations, and having found myself wedded, however unwillingly, I intended to do my duty. He then explained in a rather awkward fashion that he would prefer it if I did not act entirely out of a sense of womanly duty. I knew then that he loved me and I was content.

"That's sweet," Letty said.

"Maybe. Maybe not. I can't help wondering if Roger had finally figured out that charm would work better than a lot of loud, blustering machismo."

"I prefer to think he had learned his lesson and wanted to please Amelia."

"More likely he just didn't want to spend another night locked out of his bedroom." Kate closed the book, wondering if she would have believed Jared loved her if he had tried the same line on her.

Probably. He was, after all, the man of her dreams. He just didn't know it. She remembered their discussion over lunch a few days earlier and knew she had not been exactly truthful with him. But she was not about to confess to Jared that he was exactly what she wanted in a second husband. Not yet, at any rate.

Before this relationship could go any further she had to find a way to save him from his own piratical tendencies. She had to discover what was going on at Hawthorne Castle.

The next day she got her first real clue. It was late in the afternoon, shortly before she was due to meet Jared for dinner in the hotel restaurant, when Kate came across the most interesting portion of the diary that she had yet encountered.

Amelia Cavendish, inquisitive lady that she was, had discovered the mechanism that unlocked the hidden door at the bottom of the stone staircase.

Amelia, Kate decided as she carefully memorized the instructions, was definitely turning out to be a kindred spirit. She had been unable to resist finding out what was behind the locked wall and Kate was filled with the same gnawing curiosity.

According to the diary, Roger Hawthorne had built the hidden room as an emergency escape route to the sea. There was, according to Amelia, a wharf inside a natural cave adjoining the castle. Hawthorne had widened the entrance so that a small boat could get through to the sea and then concealed the enlarged opening with a movable section of stone that blended with the lava.

It is a very large opening, quite large enough to permit a boat to enter and dock at the small wharf inside the hidden chamber. I fear the room is not merely to be used as an emergency escape route. I believe Roger uses this secret place to unload his most valuable cargoes. I also fear these cargoes are not such as result from the honest shipping business in which he is supposedly engaged. I shall have to put a halt to such practices immediately. Roger Hawthorne is the son of an earl and I am a daughter of a respectable family. We do not indulge in this sort of thing. I will make that quite clear to him.

"Attagirl, Amelia," Kate whispered. She closed the diary and wondered more than ever if Jared was following in his ancestor's footsteps. If so, she must be as firm as Amelia had been.

NINE

"What the hell do you mean, you can't repair that railing today? Tomorrow is Thursday, remember? By tomorrow this place will be crawling with cruise-ship people. We'll need all the extra bar seating we can get. I don't want to have to block off this area just because you couldn't get the damned railing fixed in time." Fists on his hips, Jared confronted the two workmen in front of him. They both shrugged.

"Take it easy, boss," said the taller of the two. "Not much we can do without the teak. You know that. Hank said he checked over on Ruby this morning 'fore he left and it hadn't come in from Hawaii yet."

"That teak was due two weeks ago."

"Island time, boss," the second man said philosophically. "Hey, you know how it is out here. Two days, two weeks, two months. Don't make much difference. It'll get done one of these days. No hurry."

"I don't want that railing repaired one of these days, I want it fixed by this time tomorrow. I didn't get this place built by running it on island time, and

I'm not going to lose the seating capacity on that terrace tomorrow just because the damned teak didn't
leave Hawaii yet." Jared studied the broken section
of terrace railing. He was used to improvising. Out
here in the islands, a man either learned how to get
creative or he didn't survive in business.

The two workmen stood on either side of Jared, examining the broken railing with grave concern.

"Okay, Mark, I think I've got an idea," Jared finally
announced. "Remember the lumber we had left over
after we finished the new changing rooms?"

"Sure. We stored it in the back of the maintenance
shed." Mark's face lit up. "Think there's a piece that'll
fit?"

"Go check. It's not teak, but who's going to notice?"

"Right, boss."

The two men ambled off the terrace just as Letty
and David came around the corner. Letty smiled.

"Still waiting on the teak for the railing, Jared?"
Letty surveyed the broken section.

"Hi, Letty. Yeah, still waiting. Far as I can tell it
hasn't left Hawaii. The usual story. It'll get here one
of these days." He looked down at his son. "How was
school?"

"Same old thing. You seen Kate?" David's face was
screwed up with concern. "I've been lookin' all over
for her. We were gonna practice my kicks again today
and then go snorkeling."

"Haven't seen her since lunch," Jared said, deliberately quashing the memory of Kate's oddly dis-

tracted air earlier. It had irritated him because he was almost certain she was already starting to make plans for her trip back to Seattle. This was the final week of her stay and that fact was eating at him. Thus far, neither of them had brought up the subject of her imminent departure.

"Maybe she went swimming," Letty suggested.

"She wouldn't have gone down to the beach without me," David said, obviously certain of that much. "She promised she'd wait for me. She always keeps her promises."

His son was right about that, Jared thought. If Kate made a promise, she would keep it. He wondered what it would take to get Kate to promise she'd wait for him.

Then he wondered for the hundredth time how a supposedly intelligent, mature woman could entertain the silly romantic notion that she would recognize her perfect mate the moment he walked into her life. It was a particularly ridiculous and infuriating example of feminine logic and he intended to point that out to her again tonight. He himself was rapidly learning that the right person didn't always show up packaged as expected.

"She'll turn up soon. Don't worry about it," Jared told his son.

Letty smiled at David. "Your father's right. If Kate said she'd be around to work on those kicks this afternoon, then she'll be here. Why don't you go try her room again?"

David brightened. "I will. See you later, Dad."

Jared nodded. "Right. Don't forget we're going to have dinner at home with Kate tonight."

"I won't. Is she cooking again?"

"Uh-huh. Said she'd make tacos."

"Oh, boy!" David whirled and dashed off the terrace.

Letty's mouth curved in amusement. "First pizza, then hamburgers, then macaroni and cheese and now tacos. Kate certainly knows the way to a little boy's heart."

"You can say that again. If she hangs around long enough we may get hot dogs and peanut butter sandwiches." Jared made a production out of studying the broken railing. "Ten to one that's the only kind of stuff she knows how to make."

"I doubt it. But Kate's too smart to fix coq au vin or rabbit *provençle* for a kid."

"She's smart enough, all right. About some things."

"Speaking of little boys' hearts, how is yours doing?"

"I'm not a little boy, Letty."

"Oops. Sorry. Didn't mean to stomp on any toes."

"Don't worry about it." Jared heard the roughness in his own voice and stifled an oath. "My toes are tough."

"I won't worry a bit about it. You've always been very good at taking care of yourself. Time's running out, though. Are you really going to let her just up and leave in three days, Jared?" Letty wandered over to the unbroken portion of the terrace railing and leaned her elbows on the teak.

"If she wants to go home like all the rest of the tourists, there's not much I can do about it."

"I guess not. Pity, though."

"I don't need your sympathy, Letty."

"I know." She gazed out to sea. "I'm not sure it's you I was feeling sorry for. I think Kate is going to miss Amethyst. She fits in well around here, doesn't she? She's adapted very nicely to island life."

"She's stopped complaining about the lack of air-conditioning, if that's what you mean."

"Not quite. I think it goes deeper than that. The island suits her. But I suppose that's only to be expected from a woman who writes so many books featuring pirates and tropical islands."

Jared gripped the railing. "I've heard about her pirates." He paused and slanted Letty a close look. "You ever read any of her books?"

"Oh, yes. All of them. I just finished her last one, in fact—*Buccaneer's Bride*. It was wonderful. I've still got it in my purse."

Jared found himself staring at Letty's colorful, oversize canvas bag. "You do?"

Letty smiled slowly. "Umm-hmm. You know, they say you can tell a lot about an author by reading her books. A perceptive person could probably get a feel for how Kate thinks and what she fantasizes about by reading her work."

Jared swore and stretched out his hand. "Okay, let's see it."

Letty slowly unzipped the canvas bag and reached inside. "You sure you want to read a historical romance novel, Jared?"

"No, but I'm getting desperate," he admitted. He gazed down at the couple on the cover. "The heroine has red hair. Kate doesn't have red hair. She said she had something in common with all her heroines."

"Obviously it isn't her hair color," Letty said dryly. "At any rate, that's not important. Take a look at the hero and then read the first couple of paragraphs."

Jared studied the hero without much enthusiasm. "The guy needs a haircut." He opened to the first page and started to read.

His eyes were the color of the evening mist, and his hair was as dark as midnight shot with silver. There was a cruel twist to his mouth and an elegant knot in his cravat. He moved easily among the glittering guests, secure in the knowledge that Society accepted him for what he claimed to be: the wealthy, powerful Earl of Hawkridge.

But Elizabeth knew the truth about the cold and arrogant Hawkridge. Beneath his fine evening clothes the man was a pirate. Three days ago he had vowed to make her his prisoner.

Kate held her breath as she stood at the foot of the stone staircase. This was the first time she had dared to sneak back to the castle after her initial foray ten days earlier. Jared had been keeping such a close eye on her lately that Kate had begun to feel like a gold-fish in his private bowl. But today he had finally been distracted by a problem with the terrace railing. She had seized the opportunity.

She let the flashlight beam dance briefly around the small room, checking for any obvious sign that some-one else might be nearby. A heavy stillness greeted her. Then, very cautiously, she followed the instruc-tions in Amelia Cavendish's diary and pushed the metal baluster on the third step from the bottom. It gave easily—so easily that Kate knew it was kept well-oiled. But that made sense, she reminded her-self. Jared apparently used the secret room fre-quently.

There was a soft, mechanical grinding sound from deep within the stone walls and very slowly a small section opened up to reveal inky darkness.

Along with the darkness came a rush of cool air, the tang of the sea and the sound of water lapping at stone. Kate edged forward and aimed the flashlight into the hidden room.

The light bounced on the rippling surface of dark seawater then skidded a few feet to the right to reveal a short stone quay. Several large cartons were stacked beside the water. Kate stepped through the entrance and peered around with the aid of the flashlight.

She was looking at the inside of a natural cavern that had been formed aeons ago out of cooling lava. The room, as Amelia claimed in her diary, had been converted into a docking facility. She knew the cham-ber had an opening to the sea, but when she aimed the light at the far end of the cavern she saw only solid stone. Amelia's diary had not mentioned where to find the mechanism that opened the stone wall at the far end of the room.

It was clear there was plenty of room to tie up a small cruiser or similar boat here inside the hidden chamber. Back in Amelia and Roger's day, a row boat, an outrigger canoe or a sailboat could have been kept inside, ready for an emergency escape. Especially sensitive cargoes could be stored here, far from prying eyes.

There was a chill in the dark room that was not entirely from the sea. She did not want to hang around here for very long, she decided. There was something eerie about the place.

It didn't take long to convince herself that there wasn't much more to see. She darted the flashlight beam over the twisted lava walls and along the far side of the man-made quay and was about to turn back into the stairwell when she caught a glimpse of yellow at the edge of her light.

For an instant Kate went very cold. She had a sudden vision of someone lurking in the shadows of the hidden room, waiting to pounce on her. The memories of Jared discovering her the last time were all too clear.

But a few seconds later, as she still stood motionless in the opening, she realized the bit of yellow was not moving. She aimed the beam directly at it and saw a bright yellow stripe that was very familiar. It was part of a black-and-yellow wet suit.

Jeff Taylor's tanks and the remainder of his gear lay nearby.

Kate waited no longer. She backed out of the room, ran to the stone staircase and shoved hard at the baluster. The opening in the wall creaked shut.

She switched off the flashlight and bounded up the stairs.

It wasn't until she was safely outside and on the path that led back to the resort that Kate's jumbled thoughts finally slowed and settled down into meaningful patterns.

Trusting Jared was one thing. A part of her was surprisingly willing to do exactly that, though that same part did not approve of the mystery. But surely she was not obliged to blindly trust all these other people who appeared to be involved in whatever was going on around here.

Jared inhaled deeply as he walked into the cool tiled hall. The aroma of simmering taco filling emanating from the kitchen was delightful. He hadn't had tacos in ages. It made him realize how much he had missed the pleasure of walking into the house after a day's work and finding dinner cooking on the stove. Kate would probably be quick to tell him that was a sign of outdated male chauvinism. Jared decided he'd better enjoy it while he could.

There was no telling where his next all-American home-cooked meal was coming from, he realized. Unless he did something about it, he and David would be back to eating the creations of the restaurant's three gourmet chefs. That meant back to marinated goat cheese, sun-dried tomatoes and seafood pâtés. David would never forgive him.

Jared ambled into the kitchen and found it empty except for the gently steaming pot on the stove. He walked past Jolly's cage and the big bird mumbled an aggrieved squawk. Jared stopped long enough to scratch the parrot's head.

"I still say she can't bake cookies," Jared confided to the bird.

"Wanna bet?"

"No. The way my luck is running lately, I'd lose and I am not about to start losing to a birdbrain like you."

Jared headed down the hall and heard his son's voice emanating from the study. Then he heard Kate's soft, husky tones. He smiled and went to the open door.

For a moment he stood there unnoticed. David and Kate were at the desk, intently examining a drawing the boy had apparently just finished. Jared watched as his son carefully rolled up the large sheet of paper and secured it with a rubber band.

"Are you really going to frame it when you get home?" David asked, handing the rolled drawing to Kate. His eyes were large and questioning as he looked up at her.

"Oh, yes," Kate said gently. "I know a place where they frame art. It's just down the street from my apartment. I'll take it there and have them put it in a red frame and cover it with a sheet of glass. Then I'll hang it in my living room."

"Just like a real picture, huh?"

"It is a real picture. Signed by the artist, too. And no matter how much anyone offers to pay for it, I'll never sell it."

"Really?"

"Really."

Jared heard the small catch in Kate's voice and it tugged at his insides. He opened his mouth to announce his presence, but she turned her head in that moment and saw him in the doorway. The soft, damp shimmer in her eyes told him she was near tears. Even as he stared at her in stunned amazement, she blinked away the evidence.

"I'm home." Jared couldn't think of anything else to say.

"Hello." Kate didn't move. Her smile was tremulous. She clutched the rolled-up drawing as if it was very precious.

David glanced up eagerly at the sound of his father's voice. "There you are, Dad. I just gave Kate one of my drawings. She's going to frame it."

"So I hear." He smiled deliberately at Kate. "Whenever you look at it, you'll think of us, won't you?"

"Yes." She moved toward the door. "Excuse me, I've got to check on dinner."

Jared stepped aside and she slipped past him. He turned back to David, who was staring after Kate. "What's wrong, son?"

"She says she's going back to Seattle in a few days."

"That's her home, Dave."

"But she likes it here, she said so. She hasn't even complained about the heat in ages."

"A lot of people like it here, but not many of them stay. You know that."

"I bet she'd stay if you asked her to," David said, a stubborn set to his chin.

"You think so?"

David brightened. He nodded his head vigorously. "Why don't you?"

"I'll think about it." Jared smiled. "Go wash your hands. I think dinner's about ready."

Several hours later, Jared guided Kate off the dance floor and steered her out through the hotel lobby into the gardens. He was aware of a strange restlessness and a feeling of urgency. As far as he was concerned, it was all Kate's fault.

She had been moody since dinner, he reflected, and he strongly disliked moodiness in women. A man always felt he was supposed to do something about the condition and he never knew what it was he was supposed to do.

Dinner had gone well, as far as Jared could tell. Kate had been cheerful while everyone was involved in building tacos, but afterward, when they had said good-night to David and headed for the lounge, her cheerfulness had vanished like snow in the tropics.

The balmy air in the gardens soothed Jared's uncertain temper. He made himself calm down and think clearly. Letty and David were right, there wasn't much time left. In three days, Kate was going to be gone. He needed to start laying the groundwork for whatever future they had. As luck would have it, they both opened their mouths to speak simultaneously.

"Jared, I..."

"I've been thinking..."

"Sorry," he said. "What were you saying?"

"Nothing. Go ahead. What have you been thinking about?"

"Us."

She flashed him a quick, questioning glance out of the corner of her eye. "What about us?"

They were almost at the door of her room. Jared cleared his throat. "You'll be going home soon."

"Yes."

"Yeah, well, you remember I told you I get back to the States at least once a year so David's grandparents can see him?"

"I remember." She stopped and fished her room key out of her small purse.

He took the key from her. "Normally we go in August. That's a slow month around here." Jared opened the door and stood back while she entered. "But I think this year maybe we'll go a little earlier. Maybe in a month or two." He closed the door behind him.

"Is that right?" Kate did not bother to turn on a

light. She dropped her purse on the bed and kept walking out onto the veranda.

Jared moved after her, struggling for the right words. He did not know how to deal with a woman who fully expected to recognize the man of her dreams on sight, but who clearly had not done so. "Anyhow, I was thinking we could stop over in Seattle." There was no response from Kate. Jared plowed on, attempting to clarify the obvious. "We could see you." Maybe if he gave her a little time, she would come to her senses.

Kate leaned on the railing, her eyes on the darkened sea. "That would be nice," she said carelessly. "Let me know when you settle on the exact dates. I'll try to clear my calendar. Maybe we can do lunch."

Jared came to an abrupt halt. He stared at the back of her head in disbelief. *"Do lunch?"*

"Sure. Why not? For old times' sake. Assuming I'm not busy, of course."

"Do lunch." Rage boiled up inside him, hot and fierce and fueled by frustration. He crossed the short distance between himself and Kate in one long stride, grabbed her arms and swung her around to face him. "I don't believe you said that. What the hell do you mean, we'll *do lunch?*"

Her eyes locked with his, cool and distant in the shadows. "What did you have in mind? Did you plan to send David off to the Space Needle while you and I have a quick toss in the sack?"

"Dammit, you know I didn't mean it like that."

"No? Then what did you mean?"

"I thought we could see each other again, that's all."

"And I said, fine. Just let me know when you'll be in town."

"Stop making it all sound so damned casual." He released her abruptly and clamped his hands around the railing.

"But that's exactly what it is, Jared. Casual."

He looked at her through hooded eyes, trying to get a handle on whatever game it was she had chosen to play with him tonight. "It's not casual. It couldn't possibly be casual. Not for you."

"Why not?"

"Because I'm the man of your dreams." He felt the sudden stillness in her and moved in ruthlessly for the coup de grace. "You couldn't possibly feel casual about me. Not now, not ever. You might hate me or you might love me, but you would never, ever feel casual about me."

"What makes you so damned sure of that?"

He smiled thinly. "I'm reading your book. Letty gave it to me. It was a real revelation, Kate. Because I'm the hero of that book, aren't I?"

"Not very likely. I didn't even know you when I wrote it."

He shook his head, feeling more sure of his ground now. He had her on the defensive; he could feel it. Relentlessly, he stalked her. "I'm not a fool, Kate. And I'll admit I don't generally read romance novels, but it doesn't take a genius to figure out that I'm what you want and need in a man. You just haven't admitted it to yourself yet."

"Your ego is astonishing."

"Look at me, lady. Look at me and tell me I'm wrong. You want someone who is as strong as you are. You want someone who wants you so much, he can't think of anyone else. You want someone who doesn't run when you stand up to him. Hell, I even look like one of your heroes, right down to the dark hair and gray eyes. I live on a tropical island and you half believe I'm a real-life pirate. I'll bet you fifty bucks, a hundred bucks, a thousand, that you can't walk away from me without a backward glance. You're going to dream about me for the rest of your life."

Kate stared at him, her eyes wide. "The fact that you're the man of my dreams doesn't do me much good if I'm not the woman of yours."

Jared reeled. "You admit it?"

"Admit what? That you're a fantasy come true for me? Yes, I admit it. I've known it since the first time you made love to me."

Jared let go of the deep breath he had been holding. "Kate, honey, listen to me...."

"No, you listen to me, Jared." She smiled gently. "You've done enough damage tonight. I think it's time you left."

"You can't kick me out. Not now."

"I think I'd better. If I don't I'm only going to get hurt worse than I already am. I realized that this afternoon when David gave me his beautiful drawing. I've got to start pulling back."

"Kate, I don't want to hurt you. That's the last thing I'd want to do."

"Then leave."

He couldn't believe she was kicking him out. "What do you want from me?"

"Nothing."

"That's not true. You're lying. I can see it in your eyes."

"You're suddenly very perceptive for a pirate." She shrugged and leaned on the railing again. "All right, I'll admit I want something from you, but it's something I don't think you can give me, so it's better if I don't ask for it."

"Stop talking in circles. Be honest with me, Kate. That's all I'm asking."

"I'm not sure you deserve a lot of honesty. You haven't been overly honest with me, have you?"

"Kate, stop baiting me."

"All right, I'll tell you exactly what I think. I think I am in love with you, but I'm afraid of that fact precisely because you are too close to being the living image of the man of my dreams."

Heady relief washed through him. "Honey, don't be afraid to let yourself love me."

"Furthermore," she went on as if she hadn't heard him, "I think that you could learn to love me, but you're afraid to try because I'm *not* the image of the woman of your dreams."

He absorbed that in silence for a long moment. "I

hadn't thought about it that way. You think I'm so hung up on Gabriella's memory that I could never love you?"

"Not exactly, but I think that because you were happy with her, you've decided you'd only be happy again with a woman who was a lot like her. Maybe you're right. We both know I'm not at all like her, Jared. In fact, I'm her opposite in many ways. You said it, yourself: night and day."

"I don't want another Gabriella. *I don't want another angel.*" The words shocked him as much as her with their intensity. "I want a flesh-and-blood woman who understands that a man can't always be a saint. A woman who can put up with me when I lose my temper, one who won't crumple like a flower when I argue with her, one who can love me for what I am."

She stared at him, her eyes luminous in the shadows. "I want a man who can love me for what I am, a man who's not constantly searching for some image of the past."

"Maybe it's time we both stopped thinking in terms of preconceived dream images," Jared said. He touched her cheek. "I'm not still pining for Gabby. I swear it. I'll admit she left an impression in my mind of the sort of woman I could love. But that's all it was, just an impression, an idea. And you've trampled all over it. In fact, I don't think there's much left of it. When I think about the kind of woman I could love now, all I can think about is you."

Kate looked up at him, her eyes clear and deep. Jared thought he could see her heart. Her fingers closed around his wrist as he stroked the line of her cheek.

"Do you mean that, Jared?"

He framed her face with his hands and was instantly captivated by the undisguised longing he saw in her gaze. "I mean it."

He brought his mouth down onto hers, aware of an odd and unexpected rush of tenderness. She responded to it immediately, her lips softening under his, her body pressing close. For a long moment he savored the taste of her, letting himself drown in the knowledge that she wanted him. It felt so good, he thought; so right. Whatever had made him think she wasn't his type?

The tenderness caught fire and blazed into the stark need Jared always seemed to feel when he took Kate into his arms. It was exhilarating to know that he did not have to temper the force of his desire with her. He could let himself go and she would respond fully and completely. She was a woman whose passions matched his own.

"I want you, sweetheart. I've wanted you since the first time I saw you. You make me crazy, you know that?" He caught her around the waist and lifted her up off her feet. She clung to his shoulders, her green eyes brilliant with silent laughter.

"I'm glad," she said. "You do the same to me and you know it. In fact, I'm beginning to think you know entirely too much about me."

"Not a chance. I could spend the rest of my life getting to know you as well as I'd like." *The rest of my life.*

Jared lowered her until her feet touched the veranda deck. He took one step over to the lounger, sat down and tugged her tenderly down beside him.

He deliberately settled her full-length on the cushions, pushing her skirt up high on her thigh. Then he reached down, circled her delicate ankle with his hand and slowly stroked his palm upward. He loved the smooth curves of her legs and the deep, mysterious shadows that waited under the silk of her skirt. In a few minutes he would undress her and touch all those fabulous, hidden places and she would grow hot and moist with her need of him.

The anticipation made him hard. Part of him urged him to make the moment last, but another part wanted to race recklessly toward the soul-stirring conclusion. It was the devil's own choice.

"What's the matter?" Kate reached up to curl her arm around his neck, urging him close. "You look as if you can't make up your mind about something."

His answering laugh was more like a heavy groan that was torn from his chest. He started unbuttoning the bodice of her dress. "I always feel like a kid with an ice cream sundae when I'm with you. I want it all and I want it right now, but I also want to make it last."

"There's nothing that says we can only do it once," she murmured.

"Such a demanding female." Jared smiled with deep pleasure as he slipped his hand inside the open bodice. He touched the sweet curve of her breast and sucked in his breath.

Kate lifted herself against his touch, moving under his palm like a sleek cat. The honest, uninhibited desire sent the blood pounding in his veins. When she fumbled with the zipper of his jeans he shifted, gathering her beneath him so that he could lie on top of her.

He tried to undress her slowly, taking his time and enjoying every inch of skin he exposed along the way. But she kept whispering his name and sighing with such fevered longing that he knew he would not be able to last much longer. When she pushed his jeans down over his hips, leaving him wearing only his unbuttoned shirt, he decided he'd had enough of the pleasures of anticipation.

The next few minutes were hurried and a little frantic as Jared got rid of the last of Kate's clothing. He loved the way her breath quickened and her skin got slick with her excitement.

At long last Jared was where he wanted to be, sliding between Kate's legs, bracing himself on his elbow as he reached down to guide himself into her. His fingers tangled briefly in the soft hair that shielded her delicate secrets and then he was opening her gently. She cried out as he positioned himself and surged fully and deeply into her. When she closed around him he thought he would lose his sanity.

"*Jared*. Yes, please, oh, my love, please. I want you so much."

"Hold me, sweetheart. Close. Tight." The words were thick in his mouth. He was almost incoherent now as his passion roared through him. She clung to him, giving herself to him with the wholehearted generosity that never ceased to amaze him.

Jared took everything he could, knowing that even as he claimed her, he was being claimed. In those last split seconds before release he was aware of nothing except the overwhelming need to make himself a part of the woman in his arms. He had to bind her to him, make her realize that she would never be free of him.

And then Kate was convulsing gently around him, shivering exquisitely, calling to him in that soft, husky voice. Jared went rigid, hovered for an endless, mindless moment in the eye of the storm and then collapsed slowly against her.

It was a long, languid time before he reluctantly rolled to one side. He inhaled deeply, feeling his energy flowing back along his nerve endings. He could not let her leave. That was all there was to it. *He could not allow her to leave.*

"Jared?"

"Hmm?" He felt affectionate and indulgent now, the urgency and passion magically converted into a pleasant, drowsy satisfaction.

"If we're agreed that tonight marks some sort of turning point in our relationship…"

"It does. Definitely. A turning point. No casual lunches in Seattle."

"Yes, well, then I think it's time we talked honestly about a few things."

Jared immediately felt his indulgent mood begin to disintegrate. "You're going to bring up the subject of what's going on up at the castle again, aren't you? I can hear it coming. How many times do I have to tell you that it's none of your sweet business? You're just going to have to contain your curiosity and learn to trust me."

"I think I could trust you, Jared, even though I don't like being kept in the dark."

"Thanks." He felt a measure of relief at having gained that much from her, at least.

"But I see no reason why I should trust Max Butterfield or Jeff Taylor. I really feel you owe me an explanation on this."

"*Jeff Taylor*. At the castle?" Alarm shot through him, shattering what was left of his relaxed, indulgent mood. Jared jackknifed to a sitting position and grabbed Kate by the shoulders. He hauled her up to face him. "What in hell are you talking about?"

TEN

Kate was stunned by Jared's reaction. She stared up at him in shock. "What's the matter? I know you don't like me prying into this, but I really think I deserve an explanation, don't you?"

"Kate, listen to me. I'll give you all the explanations you want, but first you've got to tell me what makes you think Jeff Taylor is involved in this."

"You're not going to like it."

"That goes without saying. Just talk. And fast."

Kate drew a deep breath. "I found the secret to opening the wall in the castle."

"Where?" Jared's expression was grim.

"In Amelia Cavendish's diary."

"Damn. I should have known. All right, go on. I take it you couldn't resist going back to the castle to see if the secret worked? Never mind. Stupid question. Of course you couldn't resist. Of course you wouldn't think of doing the sensible thing and come to me to ask me about it."

"Why should I ask you?" Kate shot back, stung.

"Every time I've tried to ask you about what's going on at the castle, you tell me to mind my own business."

"Okay, okay, we'll argue about this later, I can promise you that. Right now I have to know what you saw."

"I got the wall open and I took a quick look inside. I saw some crates and cartons and the wet suit and equipment Jeff uses."

"How do you know it was Taylor's?"

"The wet suit was yellow and black. The same colors as the suit he wore diving the other day." Kate frowned. "I suppose it could belong to someone else. Does the resort rent yellow-and-black suits?"

"No." Jared released her and drove a hand through his dark hair. "What the hell is going on?"

"That's what I'd like to know. Jared, if you're involved in something illegal, now is the time to tell me. We've danced around this matter long enough."

"I've already told you, it's not illegal. But it is getting to be a damned nuisance." He stalked to the edge of the veranda and stood gazing out into the darkness for a long moment.

"Please. What is this all about?" Kate asked.

"It's about a favor I was doing for Max Butterfield."

"Max? What kind of favor?"

"It's a long story. The short version is that Max sometimes does odd jobs out here in the Pacific for the government."

"I don't get it. He's a spy or something?"

"Nothing that exciting," Jared said evenly. "Or that formal. He's not exactly on the government payroll. He's what you might call a stringer. He started out selling bits and pieces of information when he realized several years ago that he wasn't ever going to get around to writing the Great American Novel. Over the years he's had his uses, I guess."

"But what was he doing here? Why were you helping him?"

Jared reached for his jeans. "He did me a favor a couple of years back when I needed a little muscle to get rid of some rounders who decided they were going to settle here on Amethyst. He got his buddies in the department to send some professional leaners."

"Leaners?"

"Yeah. Leaners. You know. They lean on people." Jared zipped his jeans and started buttoning his shirt. "They asked a lot of pointed questions about tax-filing status and things like that. Made our unwelcome guests generally uncomfortable. They leaned until the troublemakers decided to go to some other island. The long and short of it is, I owed Max and his friends."

"And he came around to collect?"

"A couple of months ago."

"Well?" Kate followed him as he finished dressing and stepped back into the darkened room. She grabbed her dress and held it in front of her. "What did he want?"

"The guys he sells information to wanted him to set up a trap here on the island." Jared glanced over his shoulder, his mouth twisted wryly. "You should appreciate this part. Seems they were having trouble with some real modern-day pirates. Someone's got a racket going using the cruise ships."

"How?"

"They've been hijacking sophisticated electronics equipment from military and construction sites here in the Pacific. They use a small, fast boat or a plane to bring the stuff to remote islands where it's stored until the guys who are running things arrive to repackage and ship the stuff to a new destination."

"How are the cruise ships involved?"

"Max's friends figured out who was running the first stage of the operations, but they couldn't get a handle on the ringleader. The head man, disguised as an innocent tourist from one of the cruise ships, apparently arrives at the islands where stuff is stored. He takes care of business while everyone is souvenir shopping and then he leaves on the boat. In some cases the equipment is smuggled right on board."

"When a cruise ship arrives, an island like Amethyst is temporarily swamped with strangers," Kate said slowly. "It would be easy for someone to conduct some illegal activity and then leave with no one the wiser."

"Max and his pals arranged to sucker these pirates into using the hidden dock inside the castle as a temporary storage facility for the illegal shipments. They fell for it. Tomorrow when the ship arrives the boss man is supposed to hit the island and head for the castle where Max and some of his buddies are going to be waiting for him." Jared was at the door.

"Wait, where are you going?"

"To find Max. As far as I know the government people are coming in on a private plane tomorrow. There shouldn't be anyone hanging around that castle now. But apparently someone is. Jeff Taylor, if you're right about what you saw."

"You're going to tell Max something's happening there?"

"Right. This is his operation. He should know why Taylor is involved in this. I want an explanation. I don't like being kept in the dark."

"I know exactly how you feel."

Jared gritted his teeth. "I'm never going to hear the end of this, am I?" He was halfway out the door but he halted abruptly and looked back at her, his eyes intent. "Kate, listen to me. I may be busy for a while. I don't know what's going on or what's going to happen next. But if I'm not back in an hour, I want you to call Sam Finley on Ruby, you understand? The number's in the card file on my desk."

Kate was feeling more uneasy by the second. "It would take him a long time to get here."

"With any luck we won't need him at all. Max probably knows what's going on and has everything under control."

"You don't believe that or you wouldn't be acting like this. Jared, I'm worried."

Jared came swiftly back into the room and caught hold of her arms. He pulled her close and kissed her hard. When he raised his head, his silvery eyes were gleaming. "Just stay put and try not to get into any more trouble, okay? I should be back soon."

"I don't like this. Not one bit."

He flashed her a brief grin. "Look at it this way, if you hadn't gotten so curious, we'd still be out there fooling around on the veranda at this very moment. Any way you slice it, it's all your fault."

"Don't you dare blame this on me."

"Why not? Things were so calm and peaceful around here until you showed up. Nothing's been the same since you hit the island." Jared headed back to the door. "I'll be back as soon as I can."

"Jared, wait, I'm not sure this is the right—"

But it was too late. He was gone, closing the door firmly behind him.

Kate dressed slowly, her mind churning. She didn't like any of this, and most especially she had not cared for the gleam in Jared's eyes as he had walked out the door. There was enough pirate in him to enjoy this whole thing, she decided, even if he was one of the good guys.

And of course he was one of the good guys, she reflected, aware of a definite sense of relief. Her pirates might walk close to the line at times, but they always managed to redeem themselves. They adhered to their own codes of honor. When the chips were down, you could count on them.

When she had pulled on a pair of jeans and a shirt she went to stand out on the veranda. Her insides were knotted with tension. She wondered if Max was in the bar as usual and if Jared was talking to him at that very moment. Would they head for the castle? Would Max try to contact his superiors? Or would he and Jared try to take matters into their own hands?

That last possibility sent a jolt of alarm through Kate. She could just see Jared doing something like that. And if Max was in the business of dealing with modern-day pirates, he'd probably go right along with the whole stupid idea.

At the very least, they'd go up to the castle to check out the diving equipment and see what else they could find.

Kate's uneasiness grew. There was always the possibility that Jeff Taylor was at the castle himself by now. If Max and Jared walked in on him, there could be real trouble. Unless, of course, Jeff, too, was one of the good guys. But who would know until it was too late?

Kate came to a decision and headed for the door. The sensible, logical thing to do was call Sam Finley at once. Just in case.

She made her way quickly through the gardens to Jared's house where she found the lights on and the door unlocked. No one ever bothered to lock doors on Amethyst, she had learned. She let herself into the hall.

"David? Beth? Anybody home?"

"Wanna bet?"

Kate went into the kitchen. "You the only one here, Jolly?"

The bird cracked a sunflower seed and studied her

as if she were a specimen under glass. Kate gave his head a quick scratch and headed for Jared's study. The phone numbers were filed on a neat little series of cards, right where he had said they would be. Without hesitation she looked up Sam Finley's number and dialed it.

There was no answer.

Kate slowly replaced the receiver and wondered what to do next. She was getting an unshakable feeling that Jared and Max were walking into trouble. It was ridiculous to allow herself to get too nervous. Max, at least, was supposedly a professional at this sort of thing. And Jared was surely not totally devoid of common sense. But she could still picture the gleam of suppressed excitement in his eyes. Kate found herself staring at the Hawthorne dagger in the glass case.

It occurred to her that Jared had gone merrily off unarmed tonight. The dagger wasn't much of a weapon by contemporary standards, but it would have been better than nothing.

Without giving herself time to think about it, Kate opened the case, picked up the dagger and stuck it into her jeans, under her shirt. The old metal lay cold and hard against her skin. She felt a bit melodramatic, but she didn't hesitate. Her mind was made up now. She had to do something. She went to the desk and rummaged around until she found a small flashlight and then she headed for the door.

Her first stop was the lounge, but as she suspected, neither Max nor Jared was there. That only confirmed her feeling that they had both gone to the castle to see what was happening. She reminded herself that Max was apparently a pro, but that didn't kill the uneasiness she was feeling. The fact that Jeff Taylor was nowhere around did not make her feel the least bit better.

"Evening, Kate. How are you tonight?" The colonel nodded from the bar where he was busy pouring drinks for the throng.

"Fine, Colonel. Seen Jared?"

"He was in here a while ago, looking for Max. Haven't seen him since. Thought he'd be with you."

"He was earlier." Kate debated saying anything else and then decided Jared would not thank her for blabbing to the entire bar about what was supposed to be some sort of top-secret operation. "Tell him I'm looking for him if you see him," she said lamely and hurried back outside.

There was nothing else to do except go on up to the castle herself and see what was happening. If she didn't, she'd go crazy with worry.

The walk along the torch-lit path toward the beach was not too bad. But when she turned off the main trail to follow the dark path to the castle, chills shot all the way down her spine.

It seemed to take forever to reach her destination. When the tower finally loomed into view, a dark mass of stone silhouetted against a dark sky, she breathed a sigh of relief.

There was no sign of light showing through the narrow windows, but that did not tell her much. She walked quickly through the shadowed courtyard and slipped into the main hall.

It was darker than midnight inside. For a moment she stood in the doorway, listening intently. When she detected no sound at all she finally switched on the small flashlight and went over to the circular staircase.

She started down the steps with great caution. The black stairwell seemed bottomless and because of the way it twisted as it wound downward she could not see more than a few paces ahead, even with the light.

She was on the bottom step when she heard the smallest of sounds and then it was too late. A rough male arm coiled around her throat, dragging her off the step and back into the dungeon hallway. The flashlight clattered to the floor.

Frantically Kate lashed back with her foot. She was rewarded by a muffled oath.

"Hell, not again," Jared muttered in her ear. He sounded thoroughly disgusted. "I should have guessed." He relaxed his grip only slightly. "Hush. Not a sound. Not one sound."

Kate nodded quickly, the rush of adrenaline making her stomach queasy. Jared must have felt the motion of her head. Either that or he assumed she had the sense to keep quiet. He grabbed the flashlight and switched it off. Then she felt his hand close tightly around her wrist and she was being dragged deeper into the darkness behind the steps.

Kate stumbled along until Jared stopped without any warning. She immediately collided with him.

"Did you see anything at all when you came in?" Jared's mouth was next to her ear.

"No. Nothing. Can we talk in here?"

"Yes, but keep your voice down."

"I suppose it would be asking too much to turn on the flashlight again?"

"Definitely." He shifted slightly beside her but remained invisible in the pitch darkness. "What the hell are you doing here or is that a dumb question?"

"Why do you think I'm here? I tried to call Sam Finley and there was no answer. I went to the lounge and there was no sign of you, Max or Jeff Taylor. All in all, I figured things might be getting just a teensy bit out of control, so I thought I'd come see what was happening." Kate paused to catch her breath. "Jared, what *is* happening? This is getting scary."

"You were right. Things have gotten just a bit out of control. I couldn't find Max in the bar, so I decided to check out the castle myself. He was waiting for me."

"What do you mean? Max is here? Then why are we sneaking around alone in the dark like this?"

"Max was waiting for me with a gun," Jared explained patiently. "What's more, the fat little bastard took away mine and put me into the dungeon cell. Damned embarrassing."

"He took away your gun?" Kate's voice rose on a squeak. "You had a gun with you? Where did you get it?"

"I picked it up from the house before I came up here, of course. Where do you think I got it? Amethyst is a long way from the nearest 911 operator. Out here we have to look after ourselves."

"And a fine job you seem to be doing."

"Don't start nagging now. Save it for later, okay?"

"Okay, okay. I'm trying to put this together. I take it Max has turned renegade or something?"

"Or something. Looks like he's decided to quit nickel and diming the government and go for the big time. He's involved with the pirates."

Kate was shaken. "You're lucky he didn't kill you."

"He plans to. But he wants to do it at sea so he doesn't have to worry about anyone finding the body and linking him to this mess. I was put into one of the cells to wait until they're ready to move the cargo. I was going to get shipped out along with the electronics."

"Oh, Lord," Kate whispered. "He was going to kill you. How did you get out of the dungeon?"

"Roger Hawthorne was a cautious man. He'd lived through enough mutinies to know enough to plan ahead. He considered the possibility that he might someday be forced to occupy his own dungeon so he designed a way out that only he knew. He put the information into his journal. I discovered the secret years ago after I started reading the books he'd left behind."

Kate was dazed. "I can't believe this. Max a traitor and potential murderer."

"You know, I never really felt a lot of warmth for old Butterfield, but I figured since his supervisors trusted him, there was no reason I shouldn't. Just goes to show—in case anybody ever doubted it—that the government is as good at making mistakes as everyone else."

"Better, probably. Poor old Butterfield. I suppose there's no predicting what the trauma of never getting his novel into print will do to a writer's mind," Kate said soberly.

"Don't be an idiot. Max never even got the damned book written." Jared was silent for a moment, obviously deep in thought.

"What about Jeff Taylor's wet suit? Why was it in the hidden chamber earlier today?"

"Max was kind enough to fill me in on that. He said Taylor has been making regular visits to the chamber. There's an underwater entrance through a lava tunnel. He could come here any time and not risk being seen."

"That explains why he liked to dive alone."

"Right. Seems he was doing some last-minute work on those crates this afternoon and wanted to consult with Max about some details. He was in a hurry and didn't want to take the time to get back into his gear and swim out around the point and into the cove. He just left his stuff here and went down the path. It was safe enough on a one-shot basis. No one noticed him, but it's damned lucky you didn't happen to be coming up the path at the same time he was going back to the resort."

"Yes. Isn't it, though." Kate's fingers trembled.

"Your being here changes things. I was going to wait for Max and Taylor to return, but now I think our best bet is to get back to the resort and try to track down some assistance from Ruby. Sam is over there somewhere. I'll start calling around until I find him."

"Good idea. Let's get out of here." Kate put out a hand to find the wall.

"This way." Jared took hold of her arm and guided her through the darkness back to the tiny room at the foot of the stone stairs.

Kate was fumbling with the first step when she felt him go very still behind her. He tugged on her arm and she obediently stopped.

Then she heard the footsteps ringing on the stone above. Adrenaline flooded her veins all over again.

Jared was already tugging her back down the stairs. She felt him moving about in the darkness and then she heard the faint groan from deep inside the stones. She whirled around, but could see nothing. The cool rush of air and the soft sound of water told her the wall was now open.

Jared pushed Kate in front of him, urging her into the hidden cavern. She moved cautiously, relying on his knowledge of the place.

A moment later she felt the rough lava wall beneath her extended palm. Jared pushed her down until she was crouching behind an outcropping of rock.

"Don't move," he breathed into her ear. "With any luck no one will see you in the shadows."

She knew then that he was going to try to surprise whoever was coming down the staircase. "Jared, wait." She caught his hand while she yanked the dagger out of her jeans. "Here."

His hand closed swiftly around the hilt of the dagger. "You, my love, truly were meant to be a pirate's lady."

He moved away from her and Kate huddled into herself. After a moment it seemed to her she heard a faint, whispering sound near the edge of the quay, as if a body were sliding into the water, but she could not be certain.

An instant later she heard the footsteps on the staircase and then a beam from a flashlight darted into the room. It slid rapidly over the stone wharf, but did not come close to her hiding place.

Kate held her breath as a familiar figure walked swiftly into the cavern, calling out commandingly.

"Butterfield? You in here?" Jeff Taylor's voice reverberated off the cavern walls. "What's going on? Why did you open the wall before I got here? So help me, if you think you're going to get away with pulling a fast one on me the way you did on your government people, you're crazy. Nobody cheats me, Max baby. Nobody at all."

The beam of the flashlight bobbed eerily about in the darkness, but it did not find Jared or Kate. It did, however, reveal the small cabin cruiser tied up at the quay near the pile of crates and cartons.

Taylor scanned the interior of the boat and then, apparently satisfied that it was empty, he propped the flashlight on one box and began loading crates into the cruiser.

That was when Jared staged his reappearance. Kate

had to admit it was done in a suitably dramatic fashion, just like a scene out of one of her novels.

He came up out of the water only inches away from Jeff Taylor's foot. Jared had the dagger between his teeth so that his hands remained free and in the glow of the flashlight he looked incredibly dangerous. His dark hair streamed back from his forehead and his teeth flashed around the handle of the knife. In that moment he was every savage buccaneer Kate had ever created.

At the last instant Jeff Taylor sensed what was happening. He tried to jump back out of reach, simultaneously grabbing for the gun in his shoulder holster.

But he was too late. Jared had already wrapped one hand around Taylor's ankle. He jerked the man off his feet and into the water. The gun sank beneath the dark surface.

The struggle in the water was short and merciless. Even as Kate darted forward from her hiding place, Jared was subduing Taylor. By the time she reached the edge of the quay and turned the flashlight beam on the two thrashing men, she saw that Jared had the dagger's point firmly lodged near Taylor's throat. Taylor stopped struggling.

"Stand back," Jared ordered as he pulled an unresisting Taylor out of the water. "Bring me that yellow nylon line sitting in the stern of the cruiser."

Kate did as she was instructed and watched in fascination as Jared neatly bound his captive with a lot of very businesslike nautical knots.

"You're a fool, Hawthorne." Taylor looked up at

Jared with furious, sullen eyes. "You should have stayed out of this."

"Tell me about it." Jared stepped back, satisfied with his knots.

"Now what?" Kate asked.

"Now you go back to the resort and try calling Sam again."

She didn't like the expression in his eyes. "What about you?"

"I'll go find Max Butterfield," Jared said. The glow of the flashlight rendered his face in stark, chilling lines.

"No need to come looking for me, Jared." Max Butterfield spoke from the shadows of the open wall. Another flashlight beam penetrated the darkness. "I'm right here. Together with my insurance policy, of course. No, don't bother reaching for that old dagger. Leave it right where it is or someone will get hurt." He motioned with the gun in his hand.

"*Dad.*" David stood at Max's side, held fast by Butterfield's grip on his arm. The boy's eyes were huge in the shadows. "What's going on? Max said you wanted to see me right away. He said you were in trouble. Are you and Kate okay?"

"As you can see, my boy, they're just fine," Max said. "For now, at any rate. Although I am saddened to see that my rather inept friend has not fared so well. You always were a trifle too precipitous, Taylor. You're an excellent planner, but you lack creativity."

Kate felt something very cold squeeze her stomach and she could only imagine how Jared must be feeling as he realized his son was now a hostage. The carefully controlled tension in him lapped at her in waves.

"Let David go, Max." Jared gazed unwaveringly at Butterfield. His voice was very quiet. "You don't need him. Get in the cruiser and go. No one will stop you."

"Now we both know it's not quite that simple, Hawthorne." Max sounded mildly regretful. He glanced at Kate and shook his head. "A pity about your curiosity, my dear. This entire matter could have been handled far more neatly if you had not gotten involved. Now I fear it will be rather messy. But a writer's life is filled with ups and downs, is it not?"

"Your life has definitely gotten a lot more messy than most," Kate said. "What made you decide to turn traitor?"

"Such a dramatic turn of phrase, my dear. I don't quite see it that way. Remember our little philosophical discussion at poolside concerning fate? I believe I mentioned then that once in a while one is given a golden opportunity to reshape one's destiny. I have been handed such an opportunity and have decided to take it."

"You really believe your own bull, Max?" Jared asked conversationally.

"Dad?" David tried to pull free of Max's grip and looked up angrily when he was not released. "Hey, Max. Let me go. Come on, let go of me."

"Not yet, David, my boy. I'm afraid I need you to ensure your father's good behavior." Max looked at

Kate, paying little attention to his small hostage. "And also that of Ms Inskip. Come along, boy." He started to drag David toward the cruiser, motioning with the gun to urge Jared and Kate out of the way.

"I'm not going anywhere with you." David started to struggle.

"Behave yourself, boy, or I'll put a bullet through your father right now. Do you understand?" Max jerked David forward.

David looked at Jared, his small face taut with fear. "Dad?"

"Don't fight him, son," Jared said, his voice calm. "Just go along quietly, okay?"

"But, Dad, I don't want to go with Max." David was near tears as he was dragged toward the boat.

"Everything's going to be all right. When this is all over, you and Kate can practice some of those things she taught you. Remember what you learned from her?"

David blinked a couple of times and the tears were halted. He glanced at Kate and she could see awareness dawning in his eyes. She nodded reassuringly.

"You might even want to start practicing right away, Dave," Jared said.

"Yeah," said David, gathering himself.

"This is all very touching," Max Butterfield said as he started to step into the boat, "but I'm afraid we really don't have time for these sentimental farewells. Jared, go open the sea wall. Come along, David."

"I'm not going anywhere with you," David announced in the distinctly stubborn accents only a nine-year-old can manage.

"Of course you are."

"Wanna bet?" David lashed out without warning, slamming the sole of his right foot squarely against Max's kneecap.

For the next few seconds, everything happened very quickly. Max yelled in pain and surprise and lost his balance. He clutched his knee and then flailed wildly for his balance. He missed the boat and toppled with slow grandeur into the black water.

David ran straight to his father. Jared caught him close in a short, fierce hug. "You are a hell of a kid, you know that?"

"It was Kate's trick," David reminded him.

"Kate is a hell of a woman. And I am one hell of a lucky man." Jared gently pushed the boy toward Kate, who held him tightly to her. Then he walked over to the edge of the quay and stood looking down at Max, who was bobbing about and sputtering seawater.

"Jared, we've been friends for a long time." Max splashed toward the stone wall. "I ask that you consider our long acquaintanceship before you do anything rash. Consider also the cash involved here."

"I have considered it, Max. I considered it while I was locked in that dungeon cell. And I considered it very closely when you threatened Kate and my son. And after due consideration I have decided I never did like you all that much, anyway."

ELEVEN

"Furthermore, I want you to know I feel some serious errors in judgment were made around here. Serious errors that were compounded by a ridiculous macho approach to the entire event." Kate reached the end of the terrace, swung around and paced back. The morning was magnificent, as usual. Out in the bay lay the sleek, white cruise ship, its passengers still at breakfast on board. "I think it was absolutely unpardonable of you not to tell me what was going on right from the start."

"It had nothing to do with you and it was potentially dangerous. The whole thing was supposed to be a secret operation. Fat lot of good it does trying to explain the concept of *secret* to women." Jared concentrated on the repair work being done on the terrace railing. He had been concentrating on it ever since Kate had finally tracked him down that morning. "Mark, watch out for the tile. It cost me a fortune to have this stuff shipped in and I don't want it chipped."

"Right, boss." Mark and his assistant exchanged quick grins as they dutifully spread a protective cloth over the expensive Italian tile. They had been listening unabashedly to the exchange between Kate and Jared for several minutes. When they finished here on the terrace, the entire resort would know every detail of the argument.

"The very fact that it was dangerous is precisely why you should have told me what was going on."

"The idea was to keep you out of it." Jared examined the lumber that was to be used for the makeshift railing. "This isn't going to look great, but it should do the job."

Kate glowered at Jared's back. "What's going to happen to Max and Taylor?"

"Sam Finley collected them bright and early this morning. He'll turn them over to the authorities." Jared frowned at his men. "Let's get moving on this, you two. This should have been completed yesterday. Those people from the cruise ship will be pouring in here in another couple of hours. Where's the colonel? He was supposed to be digging some extra tables and chairs out of storage."

"Saw him a while ago, boss. He's working on it."

"Jared," Kate began determinedly, "I would appreciate your undivided attention. I am trying to talk to you." But it was a losing battle and she knew it. They had all gotten to bed very late last night and there had been little chance to rehash the affair. Kate had awakened bright and early this morning with every intention of doing so, but thus far she had been thwarted at every turn.

"Hi, Dad, how's the railing going?" David bounded up the terrace steps and skidded to a halt near his father.

"We're getting there," Jared said.

David grinned at Kate. "You still yelling at Dad?"

"I am not yelling at your father. I am trying to have an intelligent, coherent discussion and I am being stonewalled."

"She's yelling," Jared said.

"What does stonewalled mean?" David asked.

"Never mind." Kate turned back to Jared. "Jared, I would like to talk to you in private, if you can manage to spare a few precious minutes of your valuable time."

"Not right now, Kate. Maybe I'll have some time later to let you nag me but I've got more important things to do at the moment. Okay, Mark, let's get that new section in place and see how it fits."

"This is impossible," Kate said.

"No, I think it will be just about right." Jared studied the length of wood that had been sanded down to form the new railing. "Maybe a quarter inch more off that end, Mark."

"Right, boss." Mark picked up the power saw.

"I'm wasting my breath," Kate said. "I should have known there was no point trying to have a serious conversation about this with you. You wouldn't talk to me last night and you won't talk to me this morning. I'm beginning to get the idea you just don't want to talk to me at all."

Jared must have caught the new note of resignation in her voice. He shot a quick glance over his shoulder. "There's nothing to talk about that can't wait until after that cruise ship sails. Look, why don't you go have a nice swim in the cove? Dave, take her swimming."

"Sure thing, Dad."

Kate smiled slightly at David. "No, thanks, Dave. Maybe some other time. I think I'll go back to my room for a while."

"Good idea. Have a nice nap or something," Jared said. He grabbed hold of the railing and helped his men lock it into place. "You must be exhausted after all the excitement last night."

Kate watched him for a moment. Then she looked down at David, who was studying her anxiously. "See you later, Dave. Thanks again for the drawing." She turned and walked off the terrace.

The colonel was setting out sparkling glasses on the bar as she went through the lounge. Letty was helping him.

"Morning, Kate," Letty called. "Finished chewing Jared out for not telling you about what was going on up at the castle?"

"Yes. I'm finished."

"Well, I want you to know I'm on your side in this. Men. They think they should make all the decisions and keep the ladies in the dark. For their own good, of course."

"Now, just one minute," the colonel interrupted. "Jared was doing a favor for a government man and he had been told to keep his mouth shut. He couldn't tell Kate what was going on. He couldn't tell anyone, not even me. Give the man a little credit. He was doing what he had to do. How could he have known Butterfield had turned bad? No one knew. I heard what the government man who came over with Sam Finley this morning told Jared. He said Butterfield had always been useful and they'd never had cause to suspect him."

"Naturally you'd take Jared's side in all this," Letty said. "You're a man. Seems to me that if Kate hadn't gone up to the castle with the Hawthorne dagger, Jared might have been worse off than he already was. You can't tell me that dagger wasn't very useful."

"Excuse me," Kate murmured. "I have to be on my way. I've got a lot to do this afternoon before Hank leaves for Ruby." She gave both the colonel and Letty a fleeting smile and headed for the door.

"Oh, my goodness," Letty breathed. "Did you hear that, Colonel?"

Satisfied, Kate did not linger to hear the colonel's response. She slipped out the door and into the gardens, heading for her room.

Ten minutes later Kate had all her suitcases open on the bed. She started taking clothes out of the closet.

There were some risks a woman had to take, she told herself as she worked. And if she failed, then she failed. It was better to know the truth than to live on in false hope.

By noon, Kate had to face the fact that Jared was not going to come pounding on her door demanding that she stay on the island. Perhaps he hadn't yet heard she was leaving. Or perhaps he simply didn't care.

When she went into the restaurant for lunch she discovered it was already filled with cruise-ship people who were thoroughly enjoying the stopover on Amethyst. She wandered past the gift shop and saw that it, too, was crowded. The colonel was swamped in the bar and the extra seating on the terrace was jammed. Snorkelers and swimmers swarmed down on the beach and the resort Jeeps were busying ferrying people into town for souvenir hunting.

Obviously the owner of Crystal Cove Resort had more important things on his mind today than whether one particular guest was getting ready to fly home.

Kate ate her lunch in a leisurely fashion, chatting with the waitress and the rest of the staff. Jared was nowhere to be seen. When she wandered out into the lobby she was greeted by Lani and Jim at the front desk. They looked stunned when she asked for her bill so that she could settle it.

"You're leaving? Today?"

"On the afternoon plane to Ruby," Kate explained as she signed her name on the credit card slip.

"Jared never said anything," Jim said uneasily.

"He may not have heard yet." Kate smiled as she handed back the slip. "He's got a lot on his mind today."

"That's for sure." Jim glanced at Lani, who gave a small, helpless shrug. "We're going to miss you around here."

"A lot," Lani said, her dark eyes wistful. "Things have been much more interesting around here since you showed up. It just won't seem the same after you leave."

"I've had a wonderful time, but all good things must come to an end."

"Would you do me a favor and autograph your book for me?" Lani whipped out a copy of *Buccaneer's Bride* from behind the desk. "I just loved it."

"Of course." Kate scrawled her name and best wishes inside and handed the book back. "Thanks for asking." She turned away from the desk and walked out onto the little lagoon bridge. It occurred to her that it was hot today but she didn't mind. The heat no longer seemed to affect her much. Apparently she'd acclimated.

Two hours later she and her luggage were standing on the tarmac near Hank's twin-engine Cessna. A small group of people who were preparing to leave the island milled around, waiting for Hank to load the bags.

There was still no sign of Jared.

She had known this was going to be a risk, Kate reminded herself as she nudged one of her bags toward the pile Hank was assembling. She had gambled and she had known there was a chance she would lose. Betting was a way of life here on Amethyst, but she hadn't had a lot of practice at figuring odds. She wished the stakes weren't quite so high this time.

"You ready, Ms Inskip?" Hank asked as he started boarding his passengers.

"Yes."

Hank looked down the road that led back to the resort. "You know, I kinda thought Jared might show up this time the same way he did last time."

"He showed up the last time I was preparing to leave?"

"Yes, ma'am. Showed up and paid me the price of a seat just to make sure I'd say I didn't have room for you on board. In case you showed up here at the strip, that is. Which you didn't."

Kate smiled briefly. "I guess he didn't want me to go that time."

"So what about this time?"

Kate shrugged and walked toward the plane. "Looks like he doesn't care this time."

"That can't be right. Not from what I hear." Hank scowled. "You sure he knows you're leaving?"

"If he's paying any attention at all to what's going on around him today, he knows." Kate put one foot on the bottom step.

The roar of a Jeep engine shattered the serenity of the flight field. Hank grinned in sudden relief and turned his head to look down the road again.

"Well, well, look who's here," Hank said softly.

Kate stood on the bottom step and watched the Jeep tear through the gate and race toward the plane and the small group of people clustered around it.

Jared was at the wheel. Beside him sat David, looking very fierce.

Everyone stopped talking abruptly and turned to watch as the Jeep slammed to a halt in a cloud of dust. Jared switched off the engine and vaulted out of the vehicle. He stalked swiftly toward Kate, his expression taut with anger.

"Where the hell do you think you're going?"

"Home." Kate braced herself and lifted her chin defiantly. "It's time, Jared."

"You're not due to leave until tomorrow."

"Twenty-four hours either way isn't going to make much difference, is it?"

"Are you out of your mind? It makes a hell of a difference."

"Why? What was going to happen between today and tomorrow that's so important?"

"*I was going to ask you to marry me!*" Jared roared. "That's what was going to happen."

Kate's heart leaped, but she forced herself to stay calm. "Were you really? How odd. You couldn't even find time to talk to me this morning. And you're going to be swamped with cruise-ship people until late tonight. How were you ever going to find a spare minute in which to ask me to marry you?"

"That's my business." Jared reached up and took hold of her wrist. "Get out of the way. Hank's trying to load his passengers."

"I'm one of them."

"Not anymore you're not." Jared looked over at David, who was sitting on the hood of the Jeep.

"Come give me a hand with the luggage, Dave. Kate does not travel light."

"You bet, Dad." David leaped down and dashed forward. He was wearing a huge grin now. "I knew you'd make her stay."

Kate dug in her heels at the foot of the steps. "Jared, it isn't going to be this easy. There are one or two matters we have to deal with before any commitments are made."

"Later, Kate."

She ignored him. "First, I do not appreciate the cavalier treatment I've been subjected to today. Second, I think it's high time you stopped fooling around and told me flat out that you love me. I'm sick and tired of pussyfooting around the subject."

"I love you. Dave, get those two flight bags, will you? I'll take these suitcases. Hank, could you give us a hand? We're in kind of a hurry here."

"No problem." Hank smiled genially and bent to pick up two large suitcases.

The three males started toward the Jeep with the luggage. Kate stared after them in annoyance and then hurried forward. "Not so fast, dammit."

"Honey, I've got a resortful of people trying to spend money." Jared tossed her luggage carelessly into the back of the Jeep. "I'm too busy to stand around here restating the obvious."

"What's so damned obvious? You've never bothered to tell me you love me. How was I supposed to know?"

"You wouldn't have headed for the airport this afternoon after making sure everyone except me knew where you were going unless you were damned sure I'd come after you. Okay, you've made your point. Now get into the Jeep. I've got things to do back at Crystal Cove. If you're going to be the wife of a resort owner, you're going to have to learn that sometimes the paying guests come first."

"Your wife?" She smiled brilliantly up at him.

"Yeah, my wife. Get into the Jeep, lady. Now."

"Not until I've been properly asked. You can't just order me about as if I were one of the staff, Jared Hawthorne."

He towered over her. "Ask you? Are you kidding? I'm not asking, I'm telling you you're going to marry me. You think I'd be dumb enough to ask politely and give you a chance to say no?" He took one step forward, scooped her up into his arms and tossed her into the passenger seat. "With women like you, a man has to be assertive or he'll find himself running in circles. If you don't believe me, look at me right now. Circles within circles. I'm getting dizzy."

"Ready, Dad?" David hopped into the back seat.

"Ready."

Jared turned the key in the ignition and swung the wheel. The Jeep leaped toward the road to the combined cheers of the small crowd around the plane. Kate turned in the seat to wave goodbye to Hank, who waved back before he returned to the business of loading his passengers.

"Everything's okay now, huh, Kate?" David asked, leaning over the front seat.

She grinned and reached back to ruffle his hair. The breeze was warm with the scent of exotic flowers and the sun was so bright on the sea that it almost hurt her eyes. She felt gloriously alive and sure of herself. The pirate of her dreams had just swept her off her feet and was carrying her away to his island hideaway where he would make hot, passionate love to her just as soon as he got a spare minute. The boy in the back seat of the Jeep was going to be the son she had never had. She just knew her career would flourish because living here on Amethyst Island was going to inspire her as nothing else could ever have done.

"Yes," said Kate with complete certainty. "Everything is okay."

"Wanna bet?" Jared cast a sidelong glance at Kate.

"You got a problem, Hawthorne?" Kate smiled serenely.

"Yeah, I've got a problem. It seems to me I'm the only one who's making a public commitment around here. I've declared my love in front of a whole planeload of passengers, but I haven't heard much in the way of response from you."

"Oh," Kate said, as if it had just slipped her mind for a moment, "don't worry about it. I love you, too."

Jared laughed, his satisfaction ringing loud and clear in the crystalline island air. "Yeah, I kind of figured you did."

The telegrams arrived at ten o'clock in the morning. Margaret Lark was just switching on the kettle to make her customary morning cup of tea when her doorbell rang. She accepted the message, skimmed it hurriedly and grabbed the phone to dial Sarah Fleetwood's number.

"Did you get one, too?"

"Sure did. Can you believe it?" Sarah laughed with delight.

"No. This is incredible. What a cure for stress."

"I knew Amethyst Island was the right place to send her. I just had a feeling." Sarah carefully unfolded her copy of the telegram and reread it once more.

Have found my pirate. He's got everything: dark hair, gray eyes and a real dagger. Married yesterday. Will see you soon when we return to the States for a visit. Regards, Kate.

Take 2 of
"The Best of the Best™"
Novels FREE
Plus get a FREE surprise gift!

Special Limited-Time Offer

Mail to The Best of the Best™

3010 Walden Avenue
P.O. Box 1867
Buffalo, N.Y. 14240-1867

YES! Please send me 2 free novels and my free surprise gift. Then send me 3 of "The Best of the Best™" novels each month. I'll receive the best books by the world's hottest romance authors. Bill me at the low price of $4.24 each plus 25¢ delivery per book and applicable sales tax, if any.* That's the complete price, and a saving of over 20% off the cover prices—quite a bargain! I understand that accepting the books and gift places me under no obligation ever to buy any books. I can always return a shipment and cancel at any time. Even if I never buy another book, the 2 free books and the surprise gift are mine to keep forever.

183 MEN CH74

Name	(PLEASE PRINT)	
Address		Apt. No.
City	State	Zip

This offer is limited to one order per household and not valid to current subscribers.
*Terms and prices are subject to change without notice. Sales tax applicable in N.Y.
All orders subject to approval.

UBOB-98

©1996 MIRA BOOKS

Available in May!

National bestselling authors
JENNIFER BLAKE
EMILIE RICHARDS

Welcome to the Old South—a place where the finest women are ladies and the best men are gentlemen. And where men from the wrong side of town have more honor than all the blue bloods combined! This is a place where everyone has their place and no one dares to cross the line. But some rules are meant to be broken....

Southern GENTLEMEN

**Sweeping romance and sizzling passion...
and you will soon discover that
NOT ALL MEN ARE CREATED EQUAL.**

Available in May 1998 at your favorite retail outlet.

MIRA